To My Readers:

Hello. First, I want to say thanks for your continued support. This is not your typical romance novella. I decided to venture out and explore some very real topics in this story, while yet and still delivering a happily ever after love story. This novella touches on the subject of dating younger, same-sex relations, and polyamorous relationship.

I'm a firm believer in the notion that *you can't help who you fall in love with and everyone deserves to be loved.* I know this novella will probably upset some readers, and I may even lose some readers. I'm okay with that, because whether we want to admit it or not, this is the world that we live in today and we cannot continue to turn a blind eye to these topics which are so prevalent in our society. I have many friends and family in the LGBT family, and I do not love them any less because of who they choose to love!

This story is fiction, but this story could be a living testimony to somebody's life. Maybe it's a representation of a woman that has fallen in love with a younger man, or the young guy who has fallen in love with a man and is afraid of how their relationship will be received, or maybe a young lady that has fallen in love with another woman and is afraid of being judged. Perhaps it is an individual that is unsure who he/she loves and is being drawn in two ways or the person that believes he/she is absolutely in love with two people at the same time. Maybe this story will give someone the courage to look pass everything and focus on matters of their own heart.

I hope that you guys with get the message embedded in this story. Thanks again for your continued support. Happy Holidays!!!

~Authoress Patti Doss

DEDICATION

I dedicate this book to everyone that is looking for love this holiday season and to the ones that have found love, but are afraid to love because of how society views them. This story is for you, may it help you walk in your truth!

Remember the naked truth is always better than the best dressed lie! ~Ann Landers

EXQUISITE READS PUBLICATIONS

Finding Love at Christmas

Patti Doss

PROLOGUE

My name is Serenity. I'm a 28-year-old middle school teacher in Starkville, Mississippi. I'm 5'5, 165 pounds, honey-skinned, hourglass figure, educated, funny and classy. I have my own house and car, and no kids but I'm still single. Being an only child growing up and now being alone in adulthood can be tiresome.

After so many failed relationships, I gave up trying to find love. The fact that I haven't been with a man in the last eight or nine months was finally starting to sink in. I'm usually fine with being single, but it's something about the Christmas holiday, that makes me wish I had someone special to spend it with.

I observe parents in stores buying their kids Christmas gifts, men picking out engagement rings for their lovers, and families out together embracing the holiday season and it makes me so bitter because I want that one day. The rate that I'm going, it seems I won't ever get married. I can't even find a guy that's great enough to date, let along one I want to marry.

The only person that makes the Christmas holiday a little bearable is my best friend, Andrea. Andrea is like the sister I always wanted but never had, even though we are more than friends. Andrea is also my lover. No, I'm not gay or bisexual. At least, I don't see myself like that. I hate labels and I hate we live in a world where people try to define you by a label or as if you have to pick a side. I just love who I love and that's Andrea.

For a minute, Andrea got into the notion of labels and wanted me to label myself as to whether I was gay, straight, or bisexual. We had a big fight about it, and she moved to Atlanta. We reconciled, but I think our friendship and relationship changed from that day.

Friendships and relationships are two things that should never intertwine and I learned that the hard way.

Andrea's coming home for Christmas. I'm not sure how things are going to pan out, but it's going to be nice not having to spend the holidays alone, especially since my parents are going out of town for the holidays.

My dad is always taking my mom different places. The way he looks at her and how much he loves her, I can't wait to have a man who loves me as much as my dad loves my mom.

My parents don't know that I like men and women and honestly, I have no intentions of telling them, because my mom is already down my throat about grandbabies. The way she carries on about we waiting too long to have a baby, you would think I'm pushing forty or something.

All I want for Christmas is to be happy and maybe find love this holiday season.

ONE

SERENITY

Thank God it's Friday! I've been waiting on Friday to come like Eddie Murphy waited on Tuesday in the movie, *Norbit*! My best friend Andrea is coming home for the holidays and I'm beyond excited. She didn't come home for Thanksgiving because it was a busy time at her job at the Westin Hotel. She moved to Atlanta three month ago and we haven't had a chance to visit or hang out since she left.

Andrea has been my best friend since high school. I have other friends, associates, and colleagues whom I talk to, but none of those friendships are on the level of Andrea's and I relationship, even after she moved away. Andrea and I would text, Facebook chat, & FaceTime with each other when she was away, but it was never the same after she moved; we missed each other too much.

My heart started beating fast and a gigantic smile came across my face as I pulled into my driveway and saw Andrea's car. I was supposed to meet her at her hotel later on, but I guess she couldn't wait. By the time I made it to the door, I was soaking wet, and I'm not talking about sweat! In case I forgot to mention it, Andrea is also my lover.

We've been lovers for almost as long as we've been friends. No, I'm not gay; I just like what I like. Andrea was the first, last and only woman I've ever been with. She's the only woman I've ever *wanted* to be with, but I still love being with men as well. Andrea understood that and she understood me. Like I said before, she's my very best friend.

I hurriedly parked my car and went into the house. Upon entering, I heard Andrea singing Beyoncé's *1+1* in the shower. She has a beautiful voice, but only sings in the shower. Her mom forced her to sing in the church choir when she was younger, but once she was old enough to make her own decisions, she stopped. A lot of people thought she should have pursued a career in singing, but Andrea did not want to be a professional singer at all. She fell in love with hotel management after watching *Maid in Manhattan*. After we graduated from high school, she majored in Hotel Management while I majored in Elementary Education. She moved to Atlanta two months ago to take a position at the Westin Hotel.

As I walked into the bathroom, the fresh smell of Bath & Body Works Sweet Pea filled the bathroom and Andrea immediately stopped singing. I loved to listen to her sing, but she was still very protective of her voice. I quickly undressed and hopped in the shower with her. That's exactly how Andrea made me feel. Every time with her felt like the first time. She was even the first person that I ever kissed.

Andrea broke our kiss and pushed me against the back of the shower. She started kissing on my neck and breasts and, as the warm water cascaded down her back, her hands made their way between my legs. Her fingers danced inside of me, as I propped one of my legs up on the tub and been down low and placed my other leg on her shoulder to give her full access my wetness. She began licking and planting kisses on my pussy. I tried grabbing her head to guide her tongue inside, but she had plans of her own. She playfully bit, sucked and licked me so good that before long, my body was seizing. Her mouth covered my pussy as she sucked and swallowed all my juices until there was nothing left to savor. I pulled her face back up to mine and kissed her, tasting my juices in the process.

After our shower, Andrea sat on the bed rubbing oil over her body. The combination of the oil and water glistened on her skin, making her even more beautiful. Andrea was 5'5" with caramel skin, shoulder-length brown hair with copper highlights, and chocolate brown eyes. I quickly dressed and continued watching her massage the oil on her body. Watching her was a sight to behold. It was definitely turning me on, so I walked over, took the oil and started kissing her.

"Lie down," I whispered

She complied willingly and I began to drizzle the oil onto her chest. Once I was satisfied with the amount, I slowly massaged the oil onto her breasts and stomach before reluctantly moving on down to her hips and legs. I grabbed the oil bottle, which was now laying haphazardly on the floor beside the bed, squeezed out another large amount into my hands and began working my way back up to her pelvis. Once there, I stopped massaging her and slipped two fingers inside her while planting small kisses on her lower stomach and hips. I eased my tongue between her folds and gently licked up and down as if I was licking an ice cream cone on a hot, summer day. Fueled by her loud cries of passion, I began to plant bigger and deeper kisses on her center. My tongue danced around the inside of her pussy, making lines, circles, and numbers. With each lick, my fingers went deeper and deeper until Andrea pushed aside my hand and pushed my head deeper and deeper between her legs. Right before she was about to cum, I reached under the bed where "Victor" was waiting in my toy box. I grabbed "Victor" and slowly shoved him inside of Andrea. She gasped. Victor was thick and hard, but her body quickly adjusted to him as he moved in and out of her at various speeds. Her body went into full convulsions, so I removed Victor and let my lips savor her love nectar.

After all her juices were gone, I got up and kissed her on the lips. Andrea looked me in the eyes as if she wanted to say something but decided against it. She got up and went into the bathroom to freshen up. We planned to

go out for a nice night on the town since she was only

going to be here for a couple of days.

TWO

SERENITY

For my night out with Andrea, I decided to keep it simple with a pair of skinny jeans, a white graphic shirt that read, "I [red heart] my curves," with a red blazer and black stilettos. Andrea had on something similar: skinny jeans with a sheer yellow shirt, a royal blue blazer and colorful, floral heels.

We decided to go to Applebee's for dinner and drinks, but I stopped at Shell first to get gas. As soon as I finished pumping gas and got back into my truck, Andrea started complaining about the bag of trash that I forgot to throw away off the passenger side floor. I forgot how much of a neat freak she really was. I think she has OCD, but she won't admit it.

I was about to get out and throw the bag away, but as I started to open my door, I almost hit a young guy who was passing by.

I called out to him, "Excuse me, young man. Can you please put this in the trash for me?"

He turned around and said, "Sure, ma'am."

When he said *ma'am,* I looked at him, ready to scold him for thinking I was old enough to be a *ma'am*, but then I realized that he was just really young, but he was fine as hell. All 6'1, two-hundred and twenty dark chocolate pounds of him was draped in workout clothes and his shoulder-length dreads were pulled back, giving the perfect vision of his dark, chiseled features and dark brown eyes.

I must have been standing there not responding for a while because I suddenly noticed him retreating back. I snapped out of my daydreaming long enough to call out, "Thanks. What is your name?"

"Tray," he answered as he turned back around. "My name is Tramorris Clark, but everyone calls me Tray."

He started walking towards me and I noticed that he had a slight bow in his left leg.

I smiled flirtatiously at him.

"I'm Serenity and this is my friend, Andrea." Tray looked over my shoulder and waved at Andrea. Andrea waved back, but I sensed her attitude.

"Serenity," Tray said as if tasting my name, "That's a beautiful name."

I replied, "Thank you!"

I started to close my door, but Tray grabbed it and whispered, "I do, too."

A little puzzled, I asked, "You do what?"

Tray flirtatiously looked me up and down, from head to toe.

"I Love your curves."

18

He said it with such a confident, almost arrogant tone that let me know he was very interested.

Andrea must have heard it too because she loudly sucked her teeth with disappointment. His flirts were definitely working, but to mask the effect he was having on me, and to stop Andrea from acting a fool, I played it off.

"Boy, stop. I have nieces and nephews older than you. How old are you anyway?"

"I'm not a boy, and I'm not your nephew," he said with sexual aggression dripping off every syllable.

"I promise you that. I'm old enough. But if I am too young for you, then I understand." With that, he started walking back towards his truck.

I loved his assertiveness, and it didn't hurt that he was just so damn sexy. His skin looked so smooth, so perfect, and so beautiful. I always had a dread fetish and his dreads were turning me on in the worse way and at the worse time. His dreads were so neat; not like that dry mop look some guys be sporting.

"Tray!" I called to him. "I'm sorry. I didn't mean any harm."

He turned and came back to my truck door, saying, "Serenity, I'm grown and age is only a number."

Someone in his truck blew the horn and yelled at him to come on. Andrea let out a sigh of relief. Tray told his friend that he would only be a minute.

Tray turned his attention back to me, his aggressive demeanor replaced with a flirtatious one. "I would definitely like to finish this conversation. Can I get your number?"

I didn't know what to do. Part of me wanted to give him my number, but the other part of me did not want to give Andrea another reason to have a jacked up attitude. "How about you give me your number and I'll call you?"

Andrea relaxed a little, because she knows that normally, if I said that to a guy, it meant that I would never call them. Tray ignored Andrea snickering and gave me his number anyway. Andrea felt confident that I wouldn't give Tray a call, but as I watched him pull off, I knew that I was very interested in him.

I would definitely be giving him a call.

THREE

SERENITY

Andrea and I ended up going to Buffalo Wild Wings instead of Applebee's. The place wasn't too packed, so we got a nice table near the back of the restaurant, not far from the bar. We ordered wings, margaritas and a couple of Patron shots while we caught up on some girl talk. A group of guys came in and sat at the bar. Most of them were handsome, but there was one or two that wasn't. Andrea and I pretended we didn't see them attempting to get our attention. The waitress came over with two more Patron shots and said they were from the guys at the bar. We turned towards them and said thank you. After the waitress left, one of the guys came over and tried to holler at Andrea.

"I'm sorry but I don't date men," she told him. "But I and my *girlfriend* would like to thank you for the drinks." She then reached over and rubbed her hands on my hips. I wanted to laugh, but I didn't want to give her away. The guy's eyes got big and lit up like a kid on Christmas morning, but the look on Andrea's face smothered all his happy thoughts like the Grinch that stole Christmas. The guy finally got the picture and left. As soon as he walked off, I started laughing.

Although Andrea did what she did as a joke, she hated for guys to try to holler at us when we were together. It was one of her pet peeves. Even though we weren't in a relationship per se, she felt that it was disrespectful.

Deep down, I knew that Andrea's feelings were getting deeper for me. She was at the point where she wanted us to actually try being in a monogamous relationship. I cared for Andrea deeply, but being in a relationship with a woman exclusively was not something that I wanted.

The tequila was sneaking up on me because I was getting horny as hell, so I leaned in and whispered to Andrea to come to the restroom with me. As soon as we got to the restroom and I saw that it was empty, I pulled Andrea into the handicapped stall at the end of the bathroom. I started kissing on her neck while unbuttoning her pants, then lifted up her shirt to the view of her lovely breasts. Her 38 C breasts were running over her bra, so I just popped one out of her lace bra and began sucking on it. I pulled down her pants and thong and quickly moved my mouth from her breast to her juicy, wet pussy.

"Mmm. Yes, baby," she sung as I licked and sucked her pussy, each lick going deeper and deeper until she burst on my tongue. Then I sucked up all her juices and moved up to and kiss her on her neck and back to her breasts.

In return, Andrea started unbuttoning my pants. Before long, she was licking and sucking on me just like I had done her only moments before.

"Oooh shit," I tried to moan quietly. "That feels *so* good." Andrea was eating my pussy so good that I had to hold on to the silver bar because my legs felt like putty. I propped one leg up on the toilet, giving her more access to my pussy. Andrea went wild. She started licking me from the top of my pussy all the way to my ass. That shit felt so good that I didn't want her to stop. We heard someone come in the bathroom, but Andrea still didn't stop. I clamped my hand over my mouth to muffle my moans as she continued to devour me.

Whoever it was wasn't paying us any attention. They did their business, washed their hands and left right back out. To hurry up our little quickie session, I grabbed Andrea's head and guided it to my spot. It only took a minute before my body was seizing. Andrea licked my pussy clean and got up. We fixed our clothes, hurriedly washed our hands, rinsed our mouths and went back to our table as if nothing happened.

We finished our food, and drinks and left. Andrea was not really a drinker. She had only drunk one margarita and one Patron shot. I wasn't drunk, but I was definitely tipsy; those Patron shots had me feeling some type of way. Andrea was as much a control freak as she was a neat freak.

"I'll drive," she ordered. "You're too tipsy to drive."

Like I said, I wasn't drunk, but to avoid arguing with her, I just said okay and let her drive. When we arrived at my house, Andrea asked if I wanted her to stay the night. I told her that I was okay, that she could go on back to the hotel. I could tell that she was disappointed, but I had to put up limits with Andrea or things would become too complicated. I loved being with Andrea, but I also enjoyed being with men. I knew that I could not just be in a relationship with a woman exclusively, so I often forced space between us.

After she left, I immediately hopped in the shower to sober up a little. After I got out, I called Andrea to make sure she made it to the hotel okay. She said that she had and hurriedly got off the phone with me, which let me know she was upset that I didn't let her spend the night. The shower woke me up a little but I was still horny as hell. I did not want to call Andrea over and there was no one else to call, so like so many other lonely nights, I pulled out my bullet vibrator and pretended that it was my lover. I inserted the vibrator between my legs, up and down each side of my pussy before allowing it to rest on top of my clit. The bullet did its job and after a while, I started to cum. I turned the speed up and tried to get a satisfying orgasm. I definitely got a big one, but it still was not the same as a real man giving you a great orgasm. Unfortunately, I was still horny as hell. Tequila always has that effect on me.

I tried flipping through the channels to find something to watch, but all that was on were sexual movies and infomercials. I was about to pull out "Victor" or "Tony" to see if they can finish what my bullet started, but decided against it as Tray fell on my mind. I decided to text him and see if he would respond. To my surprise, as if he had been waiting to hear from me, he responded back right away.

Me: Hi, Tray. It's Serenity. What are you doing?

Tray: Hi, Serenity. What do normal people do at 2 a.m.? LOL

Me: I'm sorry if I woke you.

Tray: You didn't wake me. I'm up. Can't sleep. What took you so long to hit me up?

Me: So you've been waiting to hear from me?

Tray: Yeah, I have. Is that a bad thing? … So again, what took you so long to hit me up?

Me: No, I'm flattered. I'm hitting you up now so that's all that matters.

Tray: Seems like a booty call to me. LOL

Even though we were texting, Tray was reading the hell out of me. I don't know if I was that transparent or he just understood me.

Me: ☺ Really? I just thought of you, that's all.

Tray: You sure? Cause I don't mind being your booty call. Actually I'd be honored. LBVS

Me: Okay. ☺ I hear ya! Don't tempt me, Tray. I haven't had sex in about nine months.

Well, that was halfway the truth. I hadn't been with a man in nine months and that was a slip-up with this guy that I used to occasionally have sex with until I found out that he was married. How did I find out? His wife found out and started blowing up my phone. His wife kept coming for me, as if I was the one married to her!

After I told him about his wife playing on my phone, this ninja acted like I was in the wrong. I cursed him out and told him that if he or his wife ever called me again, I'd sue them both for harassment. I also reminded him to keep his dick in his pants if he didn't know how to properly cheat because people don't have time for drama anymore!

Tray responded back, snapping me out of that horrible thought of Jonathan.

Tray: All the more reason to let me come over ☺.

Me: I love your assertiveness, but I don't know you like that to be inviting you to my house and stuff.

Tray: But you want to know me. I tell you what; I'll send you a picture of my driver's license if that'll make you feel safe and you can send that to your friend, Andrea. Let her know that you are with me. Will that make you feel better?

The mention of Andrea's name started making me feel guilty so I quickly texted her.

Me: Andrea, I'm sorry about tonight. I didn't mean to hurt your feelings. You know I care for you. You also know that I don't want to be in a relationship with a woman. I love you and you know that, so please let's just enjoy what we have and keep it like it always been.
Andrea: Okay, Serenity. I'll TTYL.

I could tell she was still pissed, but I didn't care. I said my peace. Now it was up to her to accept it. But knowing Andrea, she wouldn't.

Before I could respond to Tray, I got a picture message of his driver's license along with his student ID from Mississippi State and the message: "Let me know what you want to do."

I have never had a one-night stand nor have I ever met a guy and hooked up with him on the same day, but there was something about Tray that had me considering those possibilities. He put me at ease enough to want to step outside the box. I can't lie; that young buck definitely had me open! I'm not sure if it was his spontaneity, assertiveness, or just the fact that he was fine as hell.

I care for Andrea, but she could never make me feel like that, no matter how hard she tried. I texted Tray back.

Me: 503 Court St Starkville. Don't forget to pick up some condoms ☺

Tray: Ok ☺ I live on campus, so I'll be there in like ten minutes or so!

Me: Ok, Tray. See you then.

I jumped out of bed and ran into the bathroom to freshen up. I started to put on something sexy, but opted for a night shirt with nothing underneath instead. I was a nervous wreck. I was getting butterflies in my stomach and I just couldn't sit still. I don't remember the last time, I ever got butterflies. I was about to text Tray to tell him not to come. My nerves were getting the best of me, so I went into the kitchen and downed two shots of vodka. The vodka helped a little and before I knew it, there was a knock at the door.

FOUR

SERENITY

Tray stood on the other side of my front door wearing a white A-shirt, red basketball shorts, long white socks and a pair of Nike Benassi sandals. I invited him in. "Do you want anything to drink?"

"No, thank you," he answered in a bedroom voice that sent chills down my spine.

I still had butterflies, so I figured one more shot would help calm my nerves. I went in the kitchen and took one more shot of vodka.

Feeling the burn of my liquored strength, I walked over to Tray, kissed him on his neck and started nibbling on his ear. Tray started making little moaning sounds and then he pulled my face to his and kissed me. His kisses were so soft and sweet, yet so full of passion. He wrapped his arms around my waist, bringing me closer to him. When he realized I didn't have on any underwear, he stopped kissing me, raised my nightshirt over my head and tossed it onto the floor. I stood before him in my birthday suit, watching him as he admired my body. I was not a top model, but my curves were in all the right places.

He traced the sides of my body, drawing my silhouette with his hands. He got up and kissed me on my lips, neck and ears before laying me on the sofa. His fingers slowly made their way to my throbbing pussy, his lips following in their wake. By the time his kisses reached my stomach, he had three fingers in me. My pussy was begging for his dick. He continued planting small kisses all over until his tongue and his fingers met, swimming together in my wetness; one trying to outdo the other.

"Oh my God! Fuck me, Tray!"

I wanted to feel him inside of me so bad, but Tray wouldn't bulge. He made figure eights, alphabets, zig-zags, and circles in my pussy while his fingers explored areas that hadn't been touched in months! I lost count of how many times I came, but each time I did, I squeezed my legs around his neck, trying to get him to stop. But he wouldn't stop or slow down! He had locked down on my pussy and wouldn't let go.

For Tray to be twenty-one years old, his head game was strong. Tray had me speaking languages I did not even know I knew. He finally stopped after my body convulsed for the umpteenth time. When he stopped, I seized the opportunity and pulled his face up to mine, kissing him and all my juices off his face. I sat up while pushing him down onto the sofa at the same time. As much as I wanted to feel his dick inside of me, I wanted to taste it first. I pulled his shirt off and started to pull down his shorts. He lifted up off the couch a little and helped me pulled off his shorts, giving me a view of his long, hard, gorgeous penis. Even though Tray was dark as a Hershey's bar, his dick was two-toned. The shaft was the color of a Milky Way candy bar and the head was a dark-caramel color. And did I mention how big it was? Tray's dick had to be about ten to ten and a half inches long and two and half inches thick. I couldn't wait to taste him. I started planting small kisses on the head of his penis before licking and sucking on the shaft of his dick as if I was playing the flute. Tray was squeezing my breasts harder and harder with each kiss I gave. After I had made music for a while, I guided my lips to the head of his penis and started sucking him inch by inch until his entire dick was inside my mouth. Tray let go of my breasts and grabbed my head. I continued to suck and deep throat Tray while he pushed and guided my head until I started to feel his body convulse. I slowed down until I was sure he wouldn't come.

I quickly grabbed a condom off the table and put it on him. I hopped on top of him and started to ride him. The sofa was making it hard to maneuver like I wanted to, so I told Tray to lie on the floor. He did as I asked and I mounted him again. Instead of riding him with my body very close to him, I placed my feet firmly on each side of him and squatted above him like I was about to sit down. I found his dick and guided it to my pussy. Then I started going up and down on it like I was doing squats. It hurt a little, but I couldn't stop. I felt Tray's dick all the way into my stomach. To not focus on the pain, I sped up.

"Slow down, baby," he grunted. "You're going to make me cum."

I stood up, turned around into the reverse cowgirl position and guided his dick back into me. I slowly rose up off him until only the head was inside me. Then I eased back down until all of him was in me again. I did that for a while before speeding up again.

"Damn," I breathed heavily. "This dick is so good!"

As I continued to ride him, Tray kept telling me to stop. "Babe… Stop… Shit…"

But this time, I didn't stop. I kept doing my inventive squats on his dick until his body started convulsing and his hardness turned soft.

I got up and lay on the floor beside Tray. He removed the condom and went to the bathroom to flush it. While he was in the bathroom, I went into the kitchen and got us some bottled water.

After downing most of our water, we laid back down on the floor. Tray laid on his stomach beside me and I was lying on my side.

The outside lights were twinkling in between the blind and illuminated the sweat on Tray's skin. The way his skin looked in the light made me want him once more. I started kissing up and down his back. He turned on his side to face me, and I saw his dick coming back to life. He started kissing on my chest and my breasts while his hands made their way to my pussy. Tray's finger fucked me until my body started convulsing before covering my pussy with his lips.

"Oh gawd!" I squealed.

Tray's arrogant chuckles were muffled between my legs as he sucked my clit. Then he got on top of me, reversed style, and moved backwards until we were in the position of the Cancer horoscope sign. The more he licked, kissed, and sucked on my pussy, the harder and deeper, I sucked on his dick, almost simultaneously, our bodies started seizing. I never swallowed before, but I decided to try it with Tray. Surprisingly, it was very satisfying.

Tray got up, turned around and grabbed my arms, helping me up. He grabbed another condom and quickly slid it on. He started kissing me while backing me up against the wall.

Then he picked me up. "Wrap your legs around my waist and put your arms around my neck."

I held on while he guided his dick to meet my pussy. Tray bounced me up and down on his dick until I was about to cum. I was both taken aback and full of pleasure at the same time. I knew he was muscular, but I didn't think that he could pick me up and let alone, hold me up while fucking.

Before I could recover from the orgasm, he put me down and told me, *bend over*.

Breathing heavily, I put my head down as far as I could and lifted my ass high in the air until it fell open like a broken heart. As if he was ready to mend it, Tray entered me fast, hard, and deep.

Tray was bringing out a side of me that I truly didn't know existed. He was making me do things I hadn't done in a long, long time. It was more than the fact that I was on a sexual drought before tonight. The way his body

41

was syncing and responding to mine was saying let me know that it was much more than my lack of sex.

Tray started going faster and faster. I gyrated and threw my ass back at him. Just like before, our bodies synced. Every move he made was matched with mine. Just as we were both about to explode, Tray slowed down and started planting small kisses on my lower back, making both of our bodies seize faster and harder than before.

After catching his breath, Tray got up and flushed the condom, drank the rest of his water, and spooned with me until we drifted off to sleep.

When I woke up in the morning, Tray was gone. I found a note on the table that read:

Serenity, you were sleeping so well, I didn't want to wake you. We have a game today and I have to get back to campus before our morning workouts. I enjoyed last night and I hope to see you again soon! ~Tray #79 (in case you watch the game)

I couldn't help but smile as I read the note and thought about my night with Tray. Christmas has come early for me, because Tray was definitely a gift that I'm glad I got to open!

FIVE

ANDREA

I never cared to label myself gay, bisexual, or whatever people use to identify themselves. I just like what I like and love who I love. Life is too short to live based on other's expectations or this country's obsession with labels.

Regardless of how I see myself, I think Serenity sees me as her gay friend and occasional lover, who's trying to turn her out. I'll admit that I've fallen for her, but I know she doesn't love me the way I love her.

I don't remember the exact moment I fell for Serenity, but I knew my love for her was more than just friendship ever since high school. After we fooled around in college that love grew deeper.

In college, I never told Serenity that I liked men and women. I'm not even sure if she knew back then, but while sharing some of our sexual fantasies, I found out that Serenity was curious about being with a woman. After that, everything was different. During sleepovers, or while getting dressed for parties, I started doing little stupid things like walking out the bathroom naked, undressing in front of her, bending over near or around her, and accidentally bumping into her ass or breasts.

One day, I caught her staring at my naked body. I saw my opportunity and took it. I told Serenity that she could touch it if she wanted to. When she didn't object, I walked over to her, grabbed her hand and guided it to my pussy, and I kissed her. Surprisingly she kissed me back and one thing led to another.

Before I knew it, Serenity was on the bed and my face was between her legs. She was screaming and calling out to God. I can't lie, the more she screamed, the more it turned me on. I licked, sucked, and savored Serenity until she couldn't take it anymore.

Serenity wanted to taste me, but she was nervous at first, so I walked back over to her and started kissing her all over to ease her nervousness. I laid on the bed and told her to come and kiss me. She kissed me from my lips to my chest. While she did that, I took her hand and again led it to my sauna. When her fingers explored how wet I was, it was like everything else came natural to her. Serenity was licking and sucking on my pussy so good that if I didn't know her, I would have sworn she was a lesbian. For it to be her first time, she was very skilled at eating pussy.

That was almost ten years ago, and I'm still her little secret, her side bitch. The more years pass by, the harder it gets to separate the friendship from our secret relationship. The world has become more accepting of the LGBT family and I wish Serenity would just accept the fact that she's bisexual and maybe then we won't have all this tension between us.

After all those years, I still let her use me and treat me like her little sex toy. I tried so many times to tell her how I really feel, but it never gets me anywhere. So, I try to distance myself from her in hopes of getting over her, but to no avail. I thought moving away would help, but it only made me want her more. I have tried relationships with women and men to get over Serenity, but it seems as if no one ever compares to her.

Like me, Serenity has trouble finding love, and after so many failed relationships, I thought Serenity would finally realize that I'm the only person she needs, but I was wrong. I was nothing more to Serenity but a wild fling. I was her Jody, her Tyrone, and her Bill. Hell, I was her side bitch and she doesn't even have a man!

I know I can't keep putting my life on hold, waiting on Serenity to see how much I love her and to decide if she wants to be with me or not. I hope we can remain friends. It would be a shame to lose such a good friendship, but sometimes when you love someone so much, it's hard to be

friends when you want so much more. I used to say that

having part of her was better than losing her, but I don't

feel that way anymore. I feel like it's all or nothing, and

tomorrow I'm going to have to tell Serenity exactly how I

feel.

SIX

SERENITY

Today is going by so slowly. I can't focus on anything because my mind is so preoccupied with Tray. Last night was awesome. I want to text him so badly, but something within me won't let me do it.

I managed to get some housework done before deciding to get out the house. I called Andrea to see if she wanted to go to the spa for manicures and pedicures and then to the mall.

I hope she isn't still mad about last night. I was kind of hard on her last night. I just hate how she always tries to force a relationship on me. I know she has feelings for me and a part of me has feelings for her as well, but I am not ready for a relationship with her. Honestly, I'm not sure if I ever will be ready. As much as I enjoy being with

49

Andrea, part of me was still scared to acknowledge my true feelings for her. Maybe I was afraid of the stigma of being labeled. I don't consider myself bisexual or gay; I prefer a man over a woman any day.

Andrea finally answered the phone and agreed to go. I decided I wasn't going to tell her about Tray, because it will only make things more complicated.

* * *

As soon as we sat down for pedicures, my phone vibrated. It was a text message from Tray.

Tray: Hey, sexy. How are you? Thinking of you and would love to see you tonight if possible?

Me: Hi, handsome. I'm fine. I have plans already, but if anything changes, I'll definitely let you know. Sorry!

I must have been smiling while I was texting, because Andrea looked at me and said, "You know you're cheesing hard. Somebody must have told you something good."

I started to lie to spare her feelings, but she asked so I decided to tell her. Andrea and I never kept secrets despite our complicated relationship.

"That was Tray. He wants to see me again."

Andrea look puzzled. "Tray…Tray….," she said as if she was trying to remember who he was.

"Oh, the young buck from the store? How did he get your number, Serenity?"

I knew that she would start with the questions, and I really didn't feel like going back and forth with her, so I decided to answer in a way that would give the answers to everything she needed and wanted to know.

"I saw Tray last night. He came over and stayed until early this morning." I knew she was going to be pissed but whatever.

Her demeanor changed and she could no longer hide her anger. "I can't believe you weren't going to tell me that you slept with him."

I didn't look at Andrea as she said that. Instead I responded, "I figured I'd spare you the details, plus it was a one-night thing."

Andrea looked at me, trying to read my facial expression to see if I was being sincere. Whatever she saw on my face must have satisfied her because she stopped with the questions. We finished up at the spa and decided to go to the mall.

Christmas decorations were everywhere. You would never believe that Thanksgiving was only two weeks ago. The Salvation Army had kettles on display and Christmas music was playing all over the mall. Every year, it seems that Christmas décor is displayed earlier and earlier. With Christmas being weeks away, the sales in the mall were unbelievable.

Victoria's Secret was having a huge sale, so we went there. Andrea made a slick comment about me buying lingerie for my new boo but I pretended I didn't hear her. New boo or not, she knows I love lace boy shorts. I could never resist a sale on them at Victoria's Secret. I bought some boy shorts and a few thongs with the matching bras. I also got the Love Spell, Pure Seduction, Pear Glaze, Endless Love, and the Secret Charm body collections. Andrea bought thongs with the matching bras and the Amber Romance, Passion Struck, Midnight Dare, Secret Craving, and the Strawberries and Champagne body collections.

Leaving out of Victoria's Secret, I spotted the multi-colored high-top Adidas I wanted in Journey's. The store wasn't packed so I figured we would be in and out in a few minutes if they had the size I wanted. Luckily they had my size. As the guy went to the back to get my shoes, Andrea was looking at some Jordan's. I'm not a Jordan's type of girl. I never bought Jordan shoes because of my lack of love and respect for Michael Jordan. I refuse to spend any money on a man who acts as if he despises his own race. Andrea, however, was a faithful buyer. She had to have every pair that came out and every pair that was re-released.

I went ahead and paid for my shoes and sat down on one of the little benches while she tried on shoes. That's when someone tapped me on the shoulder, so I turned around... and almost melted. It was Tray!

Andrea looked over, rolled her eyes, and quickly turned back around. I was blushing so hard that I didn't even let her little attitude interrupt what I was feeling inside. Tray looked even more handsome dressed up in his pink, white and blue striped polo shirt with some dark, perfectly fitted jeans and a pair of the newest Jordan's with a white NY Yankees cap. To top it off, he smelled so good. I stood up to greet Tray and he pulled me over to the side to talk to me. I told Andrea that I would be right back, and she waved me off as Tray and I left the store.

I became curious as he led me away from the store, by hand. "Where are we going?"

The look on his face was so devilish. "I'm just so happy to see you. I've been thinking about you all day."

Before I could respond, Tray pulled me into the men's bathroom, into one of the stalls, and locked the door. I loved his spontaneity; it was such a turn on. Tray pinned me up against the wall and tongued me down. He planted small kisses on my neck, while squeezing my ass with both of his hands. I didn't plan on having sex with Tray, but his assertive, his dreads, and his Issey Miyake cologne was making it hard for me to resist him. Good thing, I wore yoga pants with no underwear. I kissed Tray before I turned around, pulled my pants down and bent over, facing the bathroom stall door. Tray seemed shocked that I was willing to do it in the bathroom, but it didn't take long before his dick took over and made the decision for him. Tray plunged his dick in and out of me as I threw my ass back at him to speed up the quickie before someone came into the bathroom.

It was so hard to muffle my moans as he pushed his big dick in and out of me.

Damn, this boy was good!

Within minutes, Tray's body started to jerk. I moved forward, letting his dick slip out of me. Tray quickly released his load into the toilet. I pulled my pants back up, gathered my bags, washed my hands, and prepared to leave. We kissed some more before finally leaving the bathroom.

"It's good to see you," he flirted.

"Likewise, mister." I blushed. "I need to get back to the store before Andrea starts looking for me."

Luckily, we made it out of the bathroom without anyone seeing us. We got back to the shoe store and

Andrea was waiting for me outside of the store. Of course, she had an attitude. I swear, sometimes I wonder how the hell we remained friends, because her attitude was starting to become a bit too much.

"Can we talk?" Andrea asked.

"I'll see you later, baby," Tray practically sang to me.

"Bye. Talk to you later."

"Can we talk?" Andrea inquired after Tray left.

"Let's talk in the food court. I'm hungry," I said while avoiding her judgmental eyes. I was time to finally address the elephant that has been lingering in the room.

SEVEN

TRAY

Last night was perfect. Serenity had me feeling some type of way. Although it's a good feeling, it's also a scary feeling. It's hasn't been two days since we met and I already miss her. I miss kissing her and rubbing my hands all over her curvaceous and voluptuous body. Her flawless chocolate skin, dark eyes, and short hair was mesmerizing. I know that sounds crazy but from the day I met her, I felt a connection to her.

I have had plenty of one night stands; some I barely knew their names. Being a star football player, women throw themselves at you, young and old. I've met all types of women; women that want to take care of me, women that want me to take care of them, rich women, poor women, smart women, dumb women, crazy women…the list goes on and on. I didn't smash every woman I met, but, if I was interested in someone, then I may take it to another level. Even then, I wasn't a fool. I never got caught slipping; I always used protection.

I had a couple girls try to pin a baby on me, but DNA tests proved I was not the father. I may not remember real names but faces were never a problem. The way ball players were getting hit with paternity suits and rape charges, I had to be extra careful. I had a fantastic black book filled with nicknames, dates and pictures. Call me whatever you want: shady, selfish, but these girls were thirsty and always looking for a come up.

My current situation was "Juicy Lips." To be honest, I can't even remember her real name. I actually preferred the girls I dealt with to remain nameless because it made it easier to not become attached emotionally. Anyway, I met Juicy Lips at a campus party a few months back. We chatted for a while. By the end of the night, we had slept together, and like always, I used a condom. I know the condom didn't break, and I flushed the condom myself. Brothers were also getting caught up with that damn turkey baster baby shit. Every time I heard about a situation like that, it made me think about that episode of *The Game* where a chick was trying to trap Derwin and was all under the couch pillows looking for the condom. Like the old people say, everything that looks good ain't.

Last week, Juicy Lips called me and said that she was pregnant and that the baby was mine. I literally laughed at her. Of course, she got offended, but I told her DNA does not lie and to hit me up once she had the baby, so we can get a test done. Now, she calls herself stalking me and always trying to get me to come over. That's what I get for fucking with a THOT! I thought she was different but she turned out to be a money-hungry, thrill-seeking, ghetto ass chick.

Serenity was the complete opposite. I guess that's what drew me to her. The fact that she was older and more mature just made me like her even more. I didn't want to leave Serenity this morning, but I had to get back to campus. She has been on my mind ever since.

For as long as I can remember, girls always chased me. I never had to work hard to get laid or get a date; in fact, women asked me out. Serenity was different and that intrigued me. She was the first woman that actually turned me down for a date and I think that what intrigued me the most. When I saw her in the mall, I couldn't help but smile. Even though, it was still too early to really tell, just feels like Christmas this year was going to be really special.

I couldn't help but notice her friend Andrea didn't like me. She was always rolling her eyes and neck at me whenever I was around. I made a mental note to ask Serenity about it, but every time I'm around Serenity, Andrea does not cross my mind.

Running into Serenity was like a sign and it sent my mind into overdrive. She was looking so sexy that I wanted to just do her right there in the store. Instead, I just decided to holler at her for a minute, but as soon as we were alone, I couldn't keep my hands off her. I had no plans on having a quickie in the mall bathroom, but one thing lead to another, and I just had to have a piece of her. As expected, it was awesome. On our way back to the shoe store from the bathroom, I saw Juicy Lips. She passed by and looked directly at me.

I got a bad feeling in the pit of my stomach. She was up to something, I could feel it!

EIGHT

ANDREA

For a minute, I forgot I was supposed to be talking to Serenity about us. I was reminded when Tray texted her. I got mad as hell all over again. When he showed up at the store, I was burning up on the inside.

I still can't believe she spent the night with him. Serenity never did one-night stands, so for her to feel comfortable enough to sleep with Tray meant that she really liked him. From the looks of things, he liked her too.

Well, I'm tired of being number two, and it is either now or never, because I refuse to hold things in any longer.

We went to the food court and ordered the hot wings combo from American Deli. We had to wait on our order, so Serenity and I sat at one of the tables until our food was ready.

I finally broke the silence, "Serenity, I want to talk to you about us."

It was time. Hell, it's *been* time. I was nervous but I needed to have this conversation with her not for her, but for me. If I finally tell her how I feel at least, I won't have to wonder if she truly knows how I feel. So, I decided to just lay everything on the table.

"Serenity, I love you. I mean *really* love you. I've always loved you. I've loved you for years, and every time we are together that love grows more and more. The more my love for you grows, the more it seems as if you pull back. You treat me as a jump off. You use me for your pleasure and once you're done, you toss me aside. You act like I don't have feelings. Not acknowledging that I have feelings for you, doesn't make them go away. Even before we got involved with each other, you, being my best friend, knew my issues with my self-esteem, my dealing with my sexuality. I feel like you took that information and used it

64

against me. I never thought you would treat me like this, Serenity. I've allowed you to use me like everyone else in my life has. I just never wanted to admit it. I never wanted to see it, but it's true. I love you so much and you don't even care. I'm done letting you walk all over me Serenity. I'm done with everything. It's going to be hard to be friends with someone that you love, but I'm sure we will find a way to work out our friendship. As for everything else, it's clear that you and I want different things. So, that part of our relationship is over. I'm tired of the emotional roller coaster you put me on. One day, you love me, care for me, and want to be with me, then the next day, we're just friends. Well, there's more than one type of roller coaster, and I'm definitely ready to get off this ride because I'm tired of going in circles."

Serenity didn't say anything. She just sat there as if I didn't just pour my heart out to her. I wanted to see if she would say something but after three minutes or more of complete silence, she still had nothing to say. I just got up, grabbed my bags, picked up my food and left. Serenity probably cared more about how she was getting home than how I was feeling. I was done being her puppet. I'm sure Tray would give her a ride, because at this moment, I didn't want to be near her at all.

NINE

TRAY

As I entered the food court, I saw Serenity sitting by herself with this crazy look on her face. She looked like she had a lot on her mind. I wondered why Andrea wasn't eating lunch with her, but I was glad I didn't have to deal with Andrea's fucked up attitude.

I eagerly walked over to Serenity. "You okay?"

She said, "I'm okay," but she didn't look it. "Can you take me home?"

Her mind was definitely somewhere else, but I didn't want to overstep my boundaries. I called my boy, Tim, and asked if he could find somebody to pick him and my other boys up from the mall because I needed to take care of some business right away. Tim said he would call his girlfriend to pick them up. I said okay, apologized for the inconvenience and told him I'd hit him up later.

As Serenity and I left the mall, I saw Juicy Lips again. This time, I'm sure it wasn't a coincidence; this chick was really stalking me. I was going to have to get a restraining order or something against that chick before she started acting crazier! I didn't want to alarm Serenity about Juicy Lips, so I didn't say anything. We reached my car and got in. As soon as the doors closed, I leaned over to Serenity and kissed her. I kissed her long, hard, and deep, like I was trying to kiss all her problems away, and she kissed me as if she was willing to let go of them all and give them to me.

A knock on the window startled us both. I was glad the doors were locked, otherwise the person would have been able to open the door.

I looked up and Juicy Lips was standing outside my door, motioning for me to let the window down or to get out. I looked over at Serenity reluctantly. "Give me a minute to handle this."

My eyes told her that I would explain everything as soon as possible, if she would just give me a minute. Before she could respond, I got out the car to talk to my crazy ass stalker. Getting out, I noticed that she was parked directly behind me, so I couldn't leave until she moved her car. As soon as I closed the door, she starts going off! "Who is that bitch?!... What about our baby?! What about me?!"

When I didn't answer her questions, she took one of her keys and started scratching my car! I grabbed Juicy Lips, pushed her on top of my car and took her keys from her.

"Call the police!" I yelled to Serenity.

"Get the fuck off of me!" Juicy Lips was screaming and squirming, trying to get out of my grasp. But being a football player, I was way bigger than her and had her on lock.

The police arrived and Juicy Lips went into full victim mode. Crying and screaming like I assaulted her.

"I'm pregnant and he hit me!" she told them. "He scratched his own car!"

I stood there dumbfounded. I couldn't believe this shit.

One of the officers was actually believing her story, because he saw that I had her keys in my hands, but the other officer wanted to know why her car was parked directly behind mine as if she was deliberately trying to block us in.

"Officers, we messed around months ago," I started to explain to the officers. "Last week, she called me saying she was pregnant by me. After I told her the baby wasn't mine, she started stalking me."

Juicy Lips denied everything. "He's lying!"

"Officer, just please ask my friend, Serenity, what happened." I was embarrassed as hell that this all was happening in front of her, but I was sure as hell glad that she was there.

Officer number two walked over to the passenger side of the car and motioned for Serenity to get out. He asked her for her name and she proceeded to tell him what happened. After hearing Serenity's side of the story, they finally believed me.

"I want to press charges for the damage to my car and I want to get a restraining order against her for stalking me," I informed the officers. Officer number one, the one that originally believed Juicy Lips, placed her under arrest for vandalism and false pretense. It was then that I finally learned her real name was Precious Jones. The other officer gave me a copy of my incident report and told me that I'd have to come to the station to file a restraining order.

The tow truck came and removed Precious' car from blocking us in and then the officers left. I didn't leave right away; I had to talk to Serenity. I didn't want her thinking I was the type of guy that ran away from his responsibility. I don't know why I felt like I owed her an explanation, but for some reason, I wanted her to know the truth.

I took her hand and looked deep into her eyes. "I met Precious at a party, slept with her, but I used protection. Precious is pretending to be pregnant and acting like the child is mine. This happens to me all the time because I'm an athlete. My chances of going pro are causing all this craziness from women. I apologize for everything that happened and promise to make it up to you."

Surprisingly, she answered, "I accept your apology and it's okay. Everyone has a past. If I want to be a part of your present, I have to deal with your past as well."

Damn, I knew I liked this woman!

"There is nothing between Precious and I," I assured Serenity as she grabbed my right hand with her left hand and interlocked our fingers. I was relieved as I drove to the police station to press charges on Precious.

After being at the station for over an hour, then at my insurance company another hour, Serenity and I were both exhausted and hungry.

"Can I take you to dinner?"

Her smile lit up the dark and crazy day as she said, "Sure. Just take me home to change first."

I didn't need any presents under the tree for me this Christmas. Santa could just wrap Serenity up and put her under the tree for me!

TEN

SERENITY

If it's not one thing, it's another. From Andrea's meltdown to Tray's crazy ass baby momma drama, my day was going downhill really fast. I know I'm going to eventually have to talk to Andrea, but she needs some time to calm down. I'm sure she is still upset, so I sent her a quick text to apologize and told her to come over tomorrow so that we could talk. There was so much that I needed to say to her, but I didn't want to do it in the mall food court. She needed to know that I do love her, almost as much as she loves me, but I just can't be in a monogamous relationship with a woman. I like what we have and maybe I'm being selfish, but the world doesn't have to know our relationship, as long as we do.

As for Tray, he wanted to make up with dinner and drinks. I decided to give him a chance, but I still wondered how in the hell he linked up with Precious. I try to judge people, but Precious had ghetto written all over her. No respectable woman would ever get red and blond weave in her hair; nobody that wanted a decent job anyway. I hope Precious is no indication of the type of women Tray normally dates, though because I have enough drama in my own life than to worry about the drama in his as well.

***

Tray was downstairs at my house while I got dressed for our date. I decided on some black faux leather leggings with a turquoise sheer shirt with turquoise, black, royal blue, yellow, and white wedges with yellow accessories. Tray still had on his pink striped polo shirt and jeans and his retro Jordan's. I'm glad he did not change. I loved the way the pink looked on him, against his dark skin. We ended up going to *The Veranda*, one of my favorite places to eat. I guess it was one of Tray's as well. The Veranda is a southern-style fine dining restaurant not too far from the Mississippi State campus. It is secluded from the other restaurants in Starkville, MS. It's a great place to eat, nice atmosphere, wonderful food, friendly staff and excellent service.

Tray must have already made reservations because we didn't have to wait long for a table. As usual, the place was packed with older couples on date night, anniversary dinners, or just out to enjoy the weekend. There were a few college couples there but not many. We had a booth towards the back of the restaurant, which allowed for a little more privacy than the booths and tables near the front.

We ordered sweet tea, the Chesapeake Bay crab cakes and jalapeno & cheddar hushpuppies for appetizers. Tray order the grilled Maine lobster tails with bacon, corn risotto, grilled asparagus and citrus butter. I ordered the fried bayou catfish with crawfish sauce, sautéed squash and zucchini, Vardaman sweet potatoes and fried green tomatoes.

While we waited on the food, Tray told me about himself and his football career. Surprisingly, he has an identical twin brother named Tymorris, aka Tye, and he also had a younger sister named Tamara that was about to graduate high school.

Our appetizers and drinks came and Tray continued telling me about himself as we ate the appetizers. By the time our main dish came, I knew all about him, his family, and his love for football and his future plans. I learned that his father left them when he was twelve and that's when he turned to football to channel his anger. He also participates in track & field and basketball. He was the football standout and his brother was the basketball standout. Tray and Tye both graduated in the top ten percent of their 2004 graduating class. Tye was the Salutatorian and Tray graduated number three in his class. Tye played basketball in high school and even got offered a full scholarship to Mississippi State, but decided to accept a full scholarship from the University of Mississippi to major in biology. Tray's major was Business administration at MSU and he was a linebacker for the football team. In high school, he had a total of 254 tackles, 15 tackles for loss and 15 sacks his junior and senior year. His college stats were even better, and now he was considering entering the draft, but once he got into all that football jargon, I was lost. However, I could tell that he truly enjoyed the game.

I told Tray about my ex-husband Darius and how we were high school sweethearts that got married right after high school. I told him about how Darius wanted to have kids, but I wasn't ready and how Darius cheated on me and got the baby he always wanted. I told Tray about the divorce and being single over the past year. After talking about ourselves and our families, we started talking about current events, music, TV shows, etc. Tray was very intelligent and the more we talked, the more I realized just how mature he was for a twenty-one year old.

We finished dinner and ordered dessert. We decided to share the homemade peach cobbler with ice cream. I was actually having a great time with Tray and I didn't want the night to end. I asked Tray if he wanted to *Netflix and Chill*. Tray smiled and said ok. I'm sure he knew what Netflix and Chill really meant! As he drove, he reached over and grabbed my hand and interlocked our fingers. That simple act said a lot, although he didn't say a word. We stopped by Wal-Mart to get a few snacks. After we got out the car, Tray grabbed my hand again and we walked hand in hand towards the store.

By the time we got inside the store, we came face to face with Precious and some other girl. Precious looked as if she saw a ghost, but then I looked down and realized what she was looking crazy about. Precious had on a midriff shirt that showed her stomach. If that chick was pregnant, then Tray was nine months pregnant, too. Precious's stomach was as flat as an ironing board. She definitely was not pregnant! I knew she had *thot-ish* behavior, but now it was confirmed. She was definitely a T.H.O.T. She whispered something to the chick she was with and I heard one of them call out, "Bitch!" I was taught to not open mail that wasn't addressed to me. My momma didn't name me Bitch, so in my mind, she wasn't talking to me. Knowing that she was watching, I stopped and kissed Tray, right in front of her. Tongue and all and grabbed his hand again and walked back into the store. I looked back at here and smile.

She eventually got the memo and kept walking. She looked so stupid knowing that Tray had just caught her ass! Since we were in Wal-Mart, I decided to go ahead and get my Christmas tree and décor, since Tray could help me put it up. I found an inexpensive, artificial, pre-lit Christmas tree. I didn't want the traditional colors on my tree like red, gold, silver, or green. I decided on purple and gold instead.

I found some beautiful gold and purple ornaments. I also

found gold and purple poinsettias that could be placed on

the tree. For the tree topper, I found a purple glittery star. I

found some beautiful purple and gold paper for my door

and a big purple bow. I also got some clear Christmas lights

for the tree. We paid for the items and headed to the house

to watch *Netflix and chill.*

ELEVEN

TRAY

My night with Serenity was going perfect until we ran into Precious' ratchet ass in Wal-Mart. It's a good thing Serenity wanted some Redbox movies or I would have never found out about the fake pregnancy. Precious tried to start with Serenity, but Serenity just ignored her. After Serenity got her Christmas tree and decorations, we went to get some movies. I helped Serenity put up and decorate her tree and her door. The purple and gold looked really nice on the tree. I've always been used to the traditional tree filled with red and green, so it was nice seeing different colors. We ended our night at Serenity's house watching movies. We watched Kevin Hart's *Laugh at my Pain* first and we laughed until we almost cried. Being with Serenity felt so right, like we were meant to meet and be right here together, at this moment. Cuddling on the couch with her, sex didn't even cross my mind. The only thing I could think of was how much I didn't want the night to end.

We watched *This Christmas* next and the movie really got me thinking about settling down and having someone to bring home to meet my mom. I've watched that movie a million times before, but being here with Serenity, was like seeing it for the first time. Out of all the girls I have been through, I realize that none of them ever made me want to bring them home for the holidays.

Cuddling with Serenity seemed to put a lot of things into perspective. We watched movies until we both fell asleep.

When I woke up, the sun was already up and Serenity was in the kitchen cooking breakfast. I went to the bathroom to freshen up.

"Can you get my paper off of the front porch, please?" Serenity asked when I came out the bathroom.

"Sure," I said, as the smell of the breakfast cooking made my stomach growl with anticipation.

When I opened the front door, all I could do was yell, "What the hell?!"

"What's wrong?!" Serenity rushed to the door, saw what I saw and screamed also. Serenity's gray Hyundai Sonata had "BITCH" spray painted on the driver's side door with scratches from the hood to the trunk and the tires were flat. From the porch, we couldn't see the other side, but I'm sure it was equally vandalized. My car had some more scratches on it, along with the words "DOG" spray painted on the driver's side door and, like Serenity's, my tires were flat.

I told Serenity to call the police as I walked over to inspect the passenger's side of our cars and sure enough, that side was vandalized too. I knew it could only be one person and that was PRECIOUS!

The police came, took incident reports, took pictures and told us there was really nothing they could do because we hadn't witnessed her vandalizing my car. I informed the officer of the restraining order on Precious and the incident at Wal-Mart last night. Serenity was going off. The nice, quiet, conservative, well-mannered Serenity was gone and the ghetto ass SI-SI was coming out. "I can't wait to see that little bitch! I'm whooping her ass!"

The officer kept telling Serenity to calm down and to just come down to the station to complete a restraining order on Precious just to be safe. He told us that a detective will be in touch with us to investigate. By today being Sunday, there was no way we could get a rental car. We just called our insurance companies to file our claim and got back to breakfast, which was now cold. Serenity warmed up breakfast and we ate. After breakfast, I called Tim to come take us to the police station. It took us over an hour at the station and we were exhausted once we got back to Serenity's place.

"I have to get back to campus. I'll have my car towed first thing in the morning," I told her. "Are you going to be okay?"

"I'll call Andrea if I need anything or need to go somewhere."

We said our goodbyes and I watched her as she walked back into the house. As I watched her, all I could think was how much I wanted her in my life.

TWELVE

ANDREA

I watched Tray and his friend leave Serenity's house. I was parked a few doors down. I know I should have just packed my bags and went back home to Atlanta after I saw she was still with Tray.

Serenity had this crazy hold on me that I just couldn't understand. I waited hours for her to call me and apologize, only to receive a text. After riding by her house, I understood why she texted me instead of calling me. There was a black Camaro in her driveway, so I figured that it was Tray. It hurt me so bad that she just pushed me to the curb for someone she just met, knowing that I was only in town for the weekend. For the last two months, all I heard was how much she missed me, how much she missed us hanging, but Tray pops up and she just forgets all that.

I was parked outside of Serenity's house last night waiting on Tray to leave so that I could confront Serenity before I went back to Atlanta. By three a.m., I realized that Tray was spending the night, which made me more pissed off at Serenity.

I was about to leave when I saw this gray Honda park outside of Serenity's house. Two girls hopped out and proceeded to walk up the driveway near Tray and Serenity's cars. After about five minutes, the girls ran back to their car, laughing, and pulled off. I got out of my car and walked to Serenity's house. The girls had vandalized Tray's car. Good for him. He must have stood up his girlfriend for Serenity, like Serenity stood me up for him. Amazingly, they didn't bother Serenity's car. I saw two cans of red spray paint lying on the ground. I don't know why but I picked up one of the cans and wrote "Bitch" on

Serenity's driver side and passenger side door. I don't know why it felt good destroying Serenity's car, but it did. It made me feel a whole lot better. Now I understand how Jasmine Sullivan could write a song about vandalizing somebody's car. I took my keys and scratched up and down her car on both sides. The girls had flattened Tray's tires, so, to make it seem like the girls did it, I flattened Serenity's tires as well. Before I left, I picked up the other red spray can with the bottom of my shirt. When I went back to my car, I put that spray can in a plastic bag, tied it up, and then I put the other spray can on the floor to throw away later and went back to the hotel.

* * *

I tossed and turned all night. All I could think about was Serenity and Tray. The anger inside of me rose as I thought of Tray kissing, rubbing, touching, and licking on Serenity. The thought itself made me want to vomit. There were no reasons for me to be in Mississippi anymore, so I started packing my things to leave right away. As soon as the office opened, I checked out my hotel early and started to head home.

After getting breakfast, I had to make one quick stop before leaving. I stopped at the police department and gave them a statement of what I saw happen at Serenity's house with the vandalism case. I also gave them the spray can with the girls' fingerprints on it, so they would be charged for both vandalism cases.

I should have taken the route furthest from Serenity's house, but I just had to go by there one more time, that's when I saw Tray leaving with his friend. I know I should've just kept driving but I had to talk to Serenity. I had to know why she was treating me this way.

I knocked on the door, full of anxiety. When Serenity answered, her beauty took my breath away. She looked surprised to see me but let me in without speaking.

"Hi," I carefully spoke.

Then Serenity spoke back saying, "Hey."

I closed the door and followed Serenity into the living room, trying desperately to find the right words to say. I wanted to tell her everything that I was feeling. But, instead, I pulled her to me and kissed her with all my love; with everything I had in me. Serenity tried to fight the urge to kiss me back, but it didn't last long before she had grabbed my head and sucked on my tongue as I shoved it deeper into her mouth. I started kissing Serenity on her ears and neck and back to her lips. I walked her over to the couch and started to undress her. As Serenity laid on the couch in her birthday suit, all I could think about was how much I really loved her.

Normally, I would take my time and make love to Serenity, but this time I didn't. I just wanted to sex her body so good until she realizes that I am the one for her. I know it sounds crazy. You can't make people love you from sex, but I had to give it one last try. I shoved two fingers in Serenity's dripping wet pussy. She always says that she doesn't want to be with a woman, but her body was saying the opposite. I started tongue kissing on Serenity's sweet pussy, driving my tongue deeper and deeper with each kiss. Then I started sucking on her clit like I was trying to put a hickey there. Serenity was screaming and squirming, grabbing my head to make me stop. I pushed Serenity back to the arm of the couch and pushed her legs as far apart as they would go. I held them open with my hands and plunged my face into her pussy. I had Serenity's legs locked so she couldn't move. All she could do was burst for me, and she was bursting almost as fast as I could kiss her. Every time she came, I would suck up her sweet nectar until the next batch dropped.

I lost count of how many times Serenity came. I lessened my grip on her legs and drove my fingers back inside her as I continued to lick and suck on her wetness until she came one more time. I started kissing on her stomach and breasts.

Serenity started undressing me and laid me on the other end of the sofa. Then she started kissing up and down my body. Then, she put her head between my legs. Serenity made me cum as soon as she started kissing on my pussy, but that didn't stop her. She sucked up my succulent juices and kept exploring my pussy with her tongue. I thought I heard a noise or knock on the door or something, but I didn't want to stop Serenity. I figured whoever it was, would eventually get the message and leave. I put my leg on the back of the couch while my other leg hung off the couch and gave Serenity more room to navigate and explore my hidden treasure. Serenity inserted two fingers inside me and started kissing until her kisses met my fingers. Then she found my clit and just started sucking on it.

Just as I was about to cum, in walks Tray! "Serenity?!"

Serenity hopped up embarrassed and ran over to Tray. He tried to leave but Serenity wouldn't let him. While Serenity was trying to convince Tray to stay, I hurriedly put on my clothes.

"Wait! Tray, please don't leave! Let me explain!" Serenity said while pulling her shirt over her head. She grabbed Tray's hand and tried to lead him over to the couch where I was now sitting.

He resisted Serenity. "Stop, Serenity," he yelled as he tried to leave again. Serenity wouldn't let him go and instead started kissing on his neck and ear. Although, he wanted to leave, Serenity was convincing him to stay with each kiss. She tried to kiss him on the lips, but he stopped her.

Tray had this confused look on his face that I knew all too well. Even though he was pissed and probably hurt at catching her with me, like any man, the situation intrigued him. Serenity also had a power over him that wouldn't allow him to stay mad at her and, just like me, Tray had become another pawn in the game called, Serenity's Life.

As Serenity kissed him, He was obviously at a loss for words. He gave me a look that said, "Bitch!" I wanted to roll my eyes at him, but what would be the point of that? Neither one of us was willing to let Serenity go. Instead of rolling my eyes at Tray or cursing him out, I did the unexpected; I came closer to them and began to touch Tray sexually. Tray tried to pull away but the more he tried to pull away, the deeper Serenity kissed him.

Then Serenity tore her lips away from his and looked at me. "Kiss him."

Before I could kiss Tray, there was a knock at the door. Serenity got up slipped on her pants and went to the door. She opened the door and I heard someone asking for Tray.

When the guy walked in, I had to do a double take. He was 6'1 about two hundred and ten pounds, athletic build with dreads pulled into one big French braid and he looked exactly like Tray. He had on a navy polo shirt with fitted jeans and wheat colored Timberland boots. Serenity didn't tell me that Tray had an identical twin brother. If Tray and his brother had been wearing the same thing, we wouldn't be able to tell them apart. Even though Tray wasn't my favorite person, seeing his twin brother made me notice just how handsome Tray and his twin were.

Tray hopped up. "Tye, this is Serenity and that's Andrea. Guys, this is my twin brother, Tye"

Serenity and I were still in shock of how much the two looked alike that we both just waved our hands at Tye because the words wouldn't come out. Tray and Tye walked near the door to talk. I don't know what Tray said to Tye, but Tye came back into the living room and sat on the sofa besides me. Tray and Serenity started whispering and Serenity looked at me. I had no idea what they were talking about, but the way Serenity looked at me, I know it involved me. I started to feel uneasy and became fidgety.

"Calm down, ma! I don't bite, unless you want me to," Tye said with a smile almost identical to his brother. As much as I dislike Tray, his brother, Tye as making my panties moist.

I smiled at Tye and glanced back over at Serenity, only to find her and Tray kissing and making out as if Tye and I wasn't even in the same room. I must have went into a zone watching them because Tye took his hand and pulled my face towards him and without a word, he kissed me and started a river in my panties. Serenity grabbed Tray hand and started to lead him upstairs. Tye held out his hand for mine and without reserve, I placed my hand in his and we followed Serenity and Tray upstairs.

97

Once we got upstairs, Serenity took out her treasure box, opened it, and took out a handful of condoms and placed them on the nightstand and started undressing. Tray and Tye followed suit and eventually we all were standing there naked.

Serenity got in the middle of the bed and called to Tray. She began to kiss on his neck, ears, and chest. While I was watching her and Tray, Tye came behind me and started kissing on my neck and ears. Serenity stopped kissing on Tray's neck and called to me. I inserted myself between her and Tray, but Tray got up and stood beside his brother.

Standing side by side, the only difference between Tray and Tye was Tye's tattoo of a basketball and ring on his left upper arm. *Damn, they were fine as hell,* I remember thinking before Serenity turned and put her lips on mine.

Serenity continued to kiss me and whispered, "Relax, baby!"

The idea of having an audience was frightening at first, but the more Serenity kissed on me, the more I relaxed. By the time, she started sucking on my breasts and up and down my stomach I was damn near begging her to fuck me. She inserted her fingers in me one by one and after she reached three fingers, she allowed her lips and fingers to meet. Tye walked over to the head of the bed, where I was lying and put his dick in my face. Serenity stopped for a moment and looked up at me and shook her head yes. The way she was making me feel, I think I would have done anything to make her happy as long as I could be with her in this moment. I licked around Tye's dick before slowly putting him in my mouth. Tray grabbed a condom off the dresser, opened it, and walked to the end of the bed, as Serenity pulled her knees under her, without interrupting her tongue's assault on my pussy. Tray entered her while she continued to eat me out. I never imagined sharing Serenity like this but I must admit that the entire thing was like a long-lost fantasy, I didn't even know I had. Tray was fucking the shit out of Serenity. Serenity was annihilating my pussy with her tongue, and I was giving Tye the best head, I've ever given a guy. The sounds of lovemaking filled the room. Tray grabbed a hold of Serenity's waist and pumped harder and faster into her, causing a chain reaction because the harder he fucked her, the deeper and harder she licked me, making me suck Tye harder and faster. We all busted sequentially. Tray, Serenity, me, and then Tye. Tray went to the bathroom and flushed the condom, while the rest of us collapsed on the bed as after sex shocks ran through our bodies. Tray sat in the recliner, near the bed. After a few moments, Tray walked over to Serenity, who immediately started sucking his dick on one side of the bed. Tye started kissing on my neck and sucking on my bed. He laid me back on the bed as he got up and stood in front of me. He got a condom of the dresser, opened it, and put it on. He rubbed his fingers through my pussy to see if it was wet and it was. In fact, his fingers made me wetter, he plunged his dick into me as I wrapped my legs around his waist. He removed my legs from around his waist and spread them as far as they would go as he continued to grind in and out of me. I must admit that shit felt so good that I pulled Tye closer to me and started attacking his neck and chest. Tye was fucking me so good that for a minute, I forget about Serenity until she laid back on the bed and started kissing me as Tray started fucking her the same way, Tye was fucking me. I noticed that this time, Tray didn't wear a condom. After a while, Tye's body start convulsing and he filled the condom with his love nectar. When he went to flush the condom, Serenity moved up on the bed until she was close enough to suck on my right breast. I got on all four in the middle of the bed and started sucking on Serenity's breasts and kissing on her. Tray didn't stopped fucking her until he was about to cum and he immediately pulled out of Serenity and I saw his love nectar fall from his dick onto the floor.

I grabbed Serenity's waist and pulled her legs onto the bed and around to me. Serenity's head was at the foot of the bed and her legs were spread wide in front of me, in the middle of the bed. I dove right in savoring her sweet, sticky love juice. Tray and Tye sat down and was now watching me please Serenity. Since they were watching, I decided to give them a show. I straddled Serenity with my body facing the headboard. We were in the position of the Cancer horoscope and we stayed that way, until our bodies started to convulse and we had nothing else to give. I rolled off Serenity and kissed her before laying down beside her at the food of the bed. Tray and Tye got on the bed. Tray was kneeled in front of Serenity and Tye was in front of me. They propped both our legs up. Tray grabbed two condoms off the nightstand and handed one to Tye. Once they were ready, they looked at each other as if they were signaling for each other to start. Tray was fucking Serenity and Tye was fucking me, but after a few minutes, they looked at each other again and this time, they stopped and switched up. I looked at Serenity, who in turned looked at Tray to see if this is what he wanted. He shook his head at her giving her the okay. Tye was fucking Serenity and Tray was fucking me. As much as I wanted to despise Tray, his dick was making me like him more and more. I'm not even going to try to say who was better, because honestly, I really don't know. All I know is that I was having so much fun!

I see why Serenity was sprung, Tray was putting his down. Hell he brother could put it down too. Tray sped up and the faster he went, the more I grinded my hips to match his movements. Finally he came and went to flush the condom. Not too long after Tye did the same. They both came back and got in the bed with us. Serenity's back was to Tray, my back was Tye, and Serenity and I was face to face. I kissed on Serenity's neck and chest and sucked on her breast a little, before laying my head on her chest. That's the last thing I remember before I fell asleep.

THIRTEEN

SERENITY

I didn't expect Andrea to just pop up the way that she did. I didn't expect for things to happen as quickly as they did either. I was going to call Andrea and apologize for yesterday and really just be open with her like I should have done from the start. Andrea completes a part of me that no one else could understand. I didn't want to lose Andrea as a friend or lover. I love Andrea more than a sister and a best friend, but that love scares me. Out of fear, I pushed Andrea away from me and hurt her feelings because I didn't know how to deal with my own feelings for her. Andrea thinks she has problems with self-esteem, but to me, she doesn't. She is so comfortable with who she is and does not allow anyone else to define her. I've never been one to care about what people say, but part of me is still hesitant about being with Andrea, for fear of being labeled and judged.

Things are just so complicated right now, honestly. I can't decipher any of my feelings right now because as much as I loved Andrea, my feelings for Tray were getting stronger. Ever since I met Tray, I feel this weird connection to him, even though it has been such a short time. When Tray walked in on me with Andrea, I was so embarrassed, but I had to make him understand my love for Andrea and my feelings for him. The truth was, I was feeling both of them and I wanted them both in my life. Call me selfish, but I didn't want to decide between the two. Why do we always have to choose? Why can't we just love who we love and love those who love us?

After Tray didn't completely flip out about what he saw, I realized then that sometimes things work themselves out and that Tray just may be the bonding glue that holds me and Andrea together or so I thought. Just as I was about to put my plan in action for a threesome with Andrea and Tray, someone knocks on the door. Tray's twin brother, Tye was at the door. I didn't even know his brother was in town. I don't know what Tray said to him, but our threesome turned into a foursome real quick.

I don't know where we all got so much energy from, but we fucked like rabbits until we all passed out. I woke up a couple hours later. Tray and Tye was still asleep, but Andrea was no longer in the bed with us. I eased out of the bed to look for Andrea but first I had to use the bathroom. When I entered the bathroom, Andrea was sitting on the tub and it looked like she had been crying.

"Andrea, what's wrong?"

She looked up at me as more tears fell from her eyes and kissed me. She kissed me so passionately, I gasped. I knew she was hesitant about this situation with Tray and I'm sure bringing Tye into the mix was weighing on her as well. I didn't know it would affect her this much.

When Andrea finally stopped kissing me, I wiped her tears with my hands and told her, "No matter what happens, Andrea, I will always love you and I will always want you in my life. I am so sorry for making you feel as if I didn't love you. I was scared, baby. Scared of what other people would say. Scared of what other people would think about me or about us. But I don't care about that anymore. I'd rather have the whole town talk about me for loving you than to not have them talk about me and lose you. I don't know what the future holds but I know I don't want to go into it without you. I know you're not too fond of Tray, but I want him in my life too. I want him in our lives. Maybe we can be just one big happy family! I know that sounds crazy, but I can't decide. I don't want to decide."

Just then, Tray entered the bathroom. He looked from Andrea to me and realized he walked in at the wrong time. He started to apologize and walk out of the bathroom, but Andrea stopped him. She walked over to

Tray and told him, "I'm sorry for giving you such a hard time, Tray. You didn't do anything to me for me to dislike you, but from the moment we met, I knew you and Serenity connected right away. I felt like you were taking her away from me."

Tray didn't know what to say, so instead he reached down and lifted Andrea's face up to his and kissed her. I walked over to them and Tray stopped kissing Andrea and turned to kiss me. When we broke apart, Tray finally spoke, "I never planned on anything like this happening. I mean as a guy, sure I thought about having threesomes. What guy hasn't? But with you two, I see that it's more than that. I can't explain this feeling I have, but I see the love between you too. Maybe I'm being naïve thinking it's more than sex, but I hope that we can explore and see where it goes."

"What about Tye?" I asked.

"Tye has a girlfriend. He just has never been one to say no to a threesome or in this case, foursome, group sex, whatever you want to call it," Tray said with a laugh.

Andrea kissed him on his left cheek and I kissed him on the right to assure him that we are all on the same page.

Andrea and I hopped in the shower while Tray used the bathroom.

"Come join us," Serenity yelled to Tray.

Tray stripped and got in the shower with us. It was kind of clustered, but somehow we made it work.

Tray walked over to both of us and kissed from me to Andrea before he picked Andrea up and put her back against the shower wall. At first, he caught her off guard and she gasped. He kissed her from her lips to her neck, to her chests, breasts, and stomach, while his fingers danced in her pussy. The way that Tray was being so sensual with Andrea was making me feel jealous, but I couldn't be mad or jealous because this is what I wanted. I walked Tray and started kissing on his back as the water beat down on mines. Tray wrapped Andrea's legs around his waist and started fucking her. Andrea bounced up and down on his dick as if it was hers. For a minute I felt jealous again. I grabbed Tray's waist. "Turn around."

He turned around, so that his back was to the wall and I had more access to Andrea. I kissed up and down her back and I reached up and kissed Tray. Tray put Andrea down and kneeled down in front of her. He starting kissing and licking on Andrea's pussy, making his tongue go further with each lick. Andrea's moans of pleasure were turning me on. Before I could say or do anything, Tray moved Andrea behind him and he was driving his tongue up and down the walls of my pussy. After I started moaning, Tray turned once more to Andrea and shoved his dick into her. Tray wasn't going slow either. He was straight pounding his dick into Andrea. The water was getting cold, so I turned it off. Tray was so into pounding Andrea's pussy that I don't even think he noticed the water had gotten cold. I don't think Andrea even noticed.

"Fuck! Oh my God!" Andrea was moaning and squirming, but she kept thrusting her hips to meet his dick. She was enjoying Tray, whether she wanted to admit it or not. The green-eyed monster kept tugging inside me as I watched her body bow to him submissively.

Tray continued to pound her until his body started to seize and he exploded inside of Andrea. We all got out of the shower. Andrea came over to me and kissed me passionately. I guess she realized that the threesome shower scene became a twosome with her and Tray headlining.

"I'm sorry," she whispered in my ear before taking a toilet and drying me off.

"Sit on the toilet."

I did as I was told and Andrea kneeled down in front of me and put my legs on her shoulders as she ate me out. Each kiss had me going wild and for a minute I forgot about her and Tray, until my body started seizing and I opened my eyes to find him standing there watching us.

"My turn!" I said.

Andrea and I traded placed and I had her legs on my shoulders as I ate her out. As each moment between her and Tray played out in my head, my tongue went deeper and deeper into her pussy, while I stuck four fingers in and out of her until she busted all over my fingers. I removed my hands and used my mouth to clean her up. When I was finished I got up and walked over to Tray and kissed him, long, hard, and deep. He kissed me back.

"Fuck me, Tray!"

I wanted him to fuck me like he fucked Andrea. I wanted her to feel jealous like I felt. Tray did as I asked. He picked me up and sat me on the counter. He spread both of my legs really wide and bend down and kissed and sucked on my clit for a minute, before shoving his dick into me.

Tray was thrusting harder and deeper with each stroke. I felt it, Andrea felt it and if the walls could feel or talk, I'm sure they would have felt it too. Tray was fucking me like he had a point to prove and from the way things were going, he was doing a damn good job of getting his point across. I tried to match his rhythm and we fucked until we both were about to explode. Tray was about to pull out but I pulled him closer to me and made him nut inside of me.

Tray came back into the bedroom and got in the center of Serenity and I. I was on his right and Andrea was on his left. Tye was behind me. Andrea and I both laid our heads on Tray's chest and interlocked our fingers on his stomach. I looked at Andrea and mouthed the words, "I love you." Andrea replied, "I love you, too." Then she leaned in closer and kissed me. Almost simultaneously, we kissed Tray. We laid our heads back on Tray's chest, as he wrapped his arms around us and before long we all had fallen asleep.

FOURTEEN

TRAY

The smell of bacon woke me up. Everybody else was gone. I got up, showered, got dressed, and went downstairs. Serenity was cooking breakfast and Andrea was sitting on a barstool near the kitchen island. Serenity walked over to me and kissed me. To ease the tension a little, I kissed Andrea on her forehead and sat down on the barstool next to her, while Serenity finished breakfast.

The morning after is always awkward, but it's even more uncomfortable after a night like the one we had. There was no alcohol involved, so we couldn't blame it on the alcohol. Everything that happened had happened because we wanted it to. I must admit, it was amazing. I have never felt anything like that and I have had a lot of sex. I thought Serenity was a beast in the bed, but Andrea definitely was too. Considering the fact that just a day earlier, I couldn't stand Andrea and vice versa, I think I was actually starting to like her. She had some fire pussy!

I was definitely feeling Serenity, but I think I gave Andrea way more attention than I did Serenity. For a minute, Serenity got jealous even though she tried her best to hide it, but I dicked her down as well and burst in her as well because she definitely noticed that I didn't pull out of Andrea. Overall, I think we equally enjoyed ourselves. I know Tye enjoyed. He loved doing the twin fantasy thing. We did it a lot when we were in high school. He has a girlfriend, but they must be on bad terms for him to cheat on her. Tye was gone when I woke up, so I know this was just a one-time thing for him.

I could definitely see myself being in a relationship with Andrea and Serenity. Whether Andrea was willing to admit it or not, I think she was falling for me too. I can't explain how I know, but she was, I know it.

Serenity fixed everyone plates and we moved over to the kitchen table to eat. Still no one spoke a word, so I decided to break the ice. "We can all pretend last night didn't happen, but it did and I don't regret it. I enjoyed it and I could see myself doing it again."

When I said that, Andrea smiled. Serenity just looked at me, unsure of how to respond. Finally, she said, "I don't know what came over me yesterday. All I know is that I'm really feeling you, Tray, but I also love Andrea. Regardless of anything, she will always be in my life, so if you want to be in my life, you'll have to be willing to accept her into yours."

I looked over at Andrea and she looked down at her food, avoiding eye contact with me, so I looked back at

Serenity and said, "I don't have a problem with Andrea. I acted the way I acted because she didn't like me from the start, but I'm sure after last night, everybody likes everybody!"

We all giggled at that and finally the elephant was gone out of the room.

Andrea apologized to me once more and we all started to enjoy our breakfast until Serenity's phone started ringing. Serenity answered her phone and walked into the living room to talk. After a few minutes, she came back in and said that they found out who vandalized our cars. Andrea looked confused, but I was just happy to know they caught whoever messed up my car, even though I had a feeling that I already knew who it was.

As if reading my mind, Serenity blurted out, "It was Precious and that chick she was with that night we saw them at Wal-Mart. Apparently, they followed us back to my house and after we were asleep, they vandalized our cars. They admitted to vandalizing your car, Tray, but they denied doing anything to mine. After an anonymous witness saw them and their fingerprints were on the spray can, they were both charged for the damage to our cars. The officer said we could come and get an updated incident report if we need it for the insurance companies."

"This reminds me; we need to call a tow truck company to take our cars to the shop and go get rental cars."

Andrea spoke up and said, "Okay, I can take you guys to the rental place after the tow truck comes, but after that I have to get back to Atlanta." Sensing the sadness when Andrea said Atlanta, Serenity asked her, "What are you going to do? Are you going to stay in Atlanta?"

Andrea hunched her shoulders and said, "I really don't know, but I have to get back to work until I figure something out."

I felt kind of bad for Andrea because I knew she didn't want to leave Serenity. Even though we were all on good terms, she definitely was concerned about leaving Serenity to me!

I decided to ease her mind a little bit, so I told her, "Just go on back to your job, give them however much notice you need to give them, get your things settled up and move back home. Being how this three-person relationship is new to all of us, this is the point where it will make or break us and honestly, Andrea, I'm just starting to like you. I would hate to lose you so soon!"

I was trying to make them laugh, but Andrea didn't get it, so I apologized.

"I'm sorry, Andrea. I was only trying to lighten the mood because I know you are going to miss Serenity and I know Serenity is going to miss you."

Andrea replied, "I know." She looked like she was about to cry, so Serenity and I both went to her and hugged her.

The tow truck came and took our cars to the shop. Then Andrea took us to Hertz to pick up our rental cars. When we got back to Serenity's house, Andrea was preparing to head back to Atlanta.

"Can I have some time alone with Andrea?" Serenity asked me.

I could understand that, so I told her, "Sure. I'll run and get us some lunch."

I decided to get us some Zaxby's; the family special with twenty tenders, fries, Texas toasts, cole slaw, and a gallon of tea for only $19.99. As usual, Zaxby's was crowded and it took me about thirty minutes to get our food.

By the time I got back to the house, Andrea and Serenity were sitting on the couch watching TV. I put the food on the kitchen island and started to wash my hands as Andrea and Serenity walked into the kitchen. Andrea seemed more relaxed. Watching those two together made me jealous but excited at the same time. I was lucky as hell, but I had absolutely no clue as to how this type of thing works without someone feeling left out. For now, I'll have at least two weeks to think about it and work things out before Andrea moves back from Atlanta.

When we finished lunch, Andrea left to go back to Atlanta. I was surprised when she walked over and gave me a hug and a kiss goodbye. Of course, my hug and kiss was nothing like the hug and kiss she gave Serenity. I wasn't jealous of Andrea and Serenity's relationship, but I truly believe that Andrea was a little too sensitive for this love triangle. Even though, she puts up a nice façade, I'm not convinced that this is something she really wants.

I pulled Andrea to the side and we exchanged phone numbers. I told her to call me whenever she needed or wanted to talk. She put my number in her phone and said goodbye once more and left.

I headed back to campus because I had to go to football practice. I forgot to tell Andrea that I would be in Georgia on Saturday for the Falcons football game. Since I would be in town, I thought that maybe we could get some one-on-one time to see if this is really something she wants for herself or something that she is doing to please Serenity. Don't get me wrong, I like Serenity, but I also know she has a crazy, weird hold on Andrea. I just feel like Andrea is being forced into this and I'm not cool about that.

I sent Andrea a quick text as I drove to practice.

Me: Have a safe trip. Don't forget to call or text me if you want to talk. Shoot me a text when you make it home, so I'll know you made it safe and sound."

Andrea: Thanks Tray, I will.

FIFTEEN

ANDREA

I've been back home for four days now and I'm already starting to miss Serenity. Leaving Serenity this last time seemed to be the hardest thing I'd ever done. I'm glad that she finally acknowledged her feelings for me. I knew she was afraid of being labeled and I think that's why she pushed me away from her. I will admit, I wasn't too keen about sharing Serenity with Tray, but after being around him a little more and getting to know him, he is a likable guy. His brother seems cool as well. It's crazy what we would do for love.

I think I went along with Serenity's plan for a threesome/foursome because I didn't know how to tell her no. I could never tell her no, even at times when I really wanted or needed to. Serenity has that effect on everyone, especially me and Tray.

Serenity can be an attention-whore. She acts as if the world revolves around her. At first glance, you would think she is an only child the way she behaves, but she isn't. Serenity has three sisters and one brother, but because she is the baby, she literally acts as if the world is hers. Serenity got a little jealous at all the attention Tray was giving me and her entire demeanor changed when Tray ejaculated inside of me. Tray tried his best to not make me feel bad or neglected, I think that's why he gave me more attention, but I was just glad that he didn't monopolize Serenity all to himself. We all had a great time and we each had our moments. Tray was willing to accept me and for Serenity's sake, I was willing to accept him.

Tray texted me a couple hours after I left Starkville to make sure I made it home safely. We ended up texting each other for hours. Serenity also texted me and asked if I had made it yet. I told her I made it safely and that I was just relaxing trying to decide what I wanted to do. She said ok and told me to call her if I wanted to talk. Tray told me that he and some of his buddies were coming up to go to the Falcons game on Saturday. Tray invited me to the game with him, but football is not my thing, so I told him if possible, I'd see him after the game.

Serenity and Tray both wanted me to move back home. I understand that Tray wants to get to know me better, but my concern was with Serenity. From the way she has treated me over the years, I am just not sure if giving up my life to satisfy hers is worth it. How do I know she is sincere this time? How do I know that this three-way relationship is really something that I want? I had so many questions in my head, but not enough answers. My job at the W Hotel is doing well and I'm not sure if I want to really give that up to satisfy Serenity. I keep asking myself if the tables were reversed, would she give everything up for me. Would she give up her career, her life-long dream, or her independence, in a sense, for me? The answer is no. Serenity's world revolves around her. If it didn't satisfy her, she would have no part in it.

The more and more I thought about it, the more I realized that, even though I waited years for Serenity to make up her mind as to if she wanted to be with me or not, it changed me. I didn't tell Serenity that I was having doubts, but Tray seemed to sense my issue with everything. To keep my mind off of moving and things between Serenity and Tray, I picked up extra hours at work.

Tray was texting me more and more and we were actually getting to know each other better. He was a very interesting person, so mature for his age.

It was a pretty busy day at work. The W Hotel had a lot of events planned for the weekend. I had to finish the Christmas decorations and put the finishing touches on our lobby's Christmas tree. The W Hotel was big on tradition and the company only wanted traditional Christmas colors. So I used red and gold Christmas décor that went beautifully with the décor of the lobby area.

By the time I finished with everything and took my lunch break, it was almost three o' clock. I was in my office eating chips, when Shaundra, the front desk clerk, called me and said that I had to sign for a delivery. When I walked out of my office to the front desk, I didn't see any boxes anywhere. I was just about to scold her when I saw a delivery guy with a bouquet so big that it covered up his face.

He walked over to the front counter and asked for Andrea Lee.

"I am Andrea," I replied.

He slowly moved the flowers down exposing his face and said, "Then these are for you," and started laughing. It was Tray! I came from behind the counter and kissed Tray as he placed the flowers down. He got me good. I didn't know he was coming into town a day early and the flowers were beautiful. Shaundra cleared her throat and snapped me out of my euphoric moment.

"I'll be right back," I told Tray as I grabbed the bouquet and placed them on my desk in the office. Then I grabbed my purse and locked my office door.

"I'm still on lunch, Shaundra," I told her as I sashayed by. "I'll be back."

I was going to take Tray to Gladys' Chicken & Waffles, but I decided on something else for lunch. I told him that I needed to stop by my apartment to get something. As soon as we got inside the apartment, I was on him. I had forty-five minutes before my lunch break was over and I decided to make use of every minute. I pushed Tray's back against the door and kissed him while unbuckling his pants. Pulling his pants and boxers down to his ankles, I took him in my mouth. Instead of sucking Tray slowly, sensually and passionately, I sucked Tray like a more assertive, wild, porn star. Within seconds, Tray was moaning and grabbing my head to slow me down. Tray's body started seizing. He tried to pull out of my mouth, but I sucked harder and faster, until he came, his hot, sweet nectar shooting down my throat. I got up, quickly undressed and got on all fours. I put my head down and lifted my ass up to meet Tray as he kneeled down behind me. He plunged his dick into my throbbing pussy and began to hammer in and out of me. I caught onto his rhythm and whenever he stroked in, I threw my ass back to meet him. We went back and forth like that until his body started to jerk. I knew he was about to cum but instead of pulling out, he pulled me closer to him and let his sweet juices loose inside of me before we both collapsed onto the floor.

After a few minutes, I went to the bathroom to freshen up and get dressed so that I could return to work. When I came out, Tray was already dressed and ready to go. He walked over to me and kissed me long, hard, and deep. "What I wouldn't give for round two," I said into his mouth as we kissed. "But I have to get back to work because I missed Monday, when I stayed that extra day in Mississippi."

I dropped Tray off at his car and went back to work. When I walked in, Shaundra whispered, "Ummm hummm!" and giggled. I walked past her into my office like I hadn't heard her. Tray had me floating on cloud nine. I must say, being with him one-on-one was way better than sharing him with Serenity.

* * *

After getting off work, Tray wanted me to hang out with him, since the guys he came with were visiting friends and family members. I decided to take Tray to Stilettos, one of Atlanta's newest and hottest strip clubs. It's not overcome with wannabe thugs, broke down self-proclaimed pimps, and independent or one-hit wonder rappers like Magic City and a few of the other gentlemen clubs.

For the club, I decided on black faux leather tights with leopard print, knee-high stiletto boots and a red sheer top with a leopard print bra. Tray changed into a short-sleeved, black military style shirt, fitted dark blue jeans and some black Timberland boots.

When we arrived at the party, Tray went and ordered us some drinks while I found us a table. Before long, "Diamonique," one of the club's thick dancers, came by our table. I called her over saying, "Give my friend a lap dance." Lap dances were twenty, but I gave her fifty as Ciara's *Body Party* started to play. Diamonique was a beautiful light-skinned dancer, about 6'0" with her four-inch heels on and a shoulder-length red wig that was cut into a sleek bob. She wore a leopard print strappy pucker back monokini with red stilettos. It was weird how her attire matched almost perfectly with mine.

Diamonique started grinding and moving her body sensually and passionately on Tray's as if she was Ciara herself. Watching her ass bounce and twerk all over Tray was making me hot! The song finally stopped and *Skin* by Rihanna started to play. Diamonique was about to leave when I pulled out another fifty and told her, "Dance for me."

She started to dance for me and her body felt so damn good against mine. For a minute, I thought about Serenity and how good her body always felt next to mine. I could tell Tray was turned on by the way he watched Diamonique bounce and twerk her body on me.

Finally the song stopped and Diamonique left.

I moved closer to Tray and kissed him. "Does Serenity know about us spending this weekend together?"

"I told her that I was going out of town with some of the boys, but I didn't tell her where."

"So are you going to tell her we hooked up this weekend?"

Tray looked at me and with a straight face and said, "No."

I wanted to ask why, but something told me to just go with the flow. I said, "Okay," and went back to watching a stripper that was now on stage dancing to Twister's *Daddy!*

After a couple more hours in the club, many lap dances and a couple hundred dollars later, I was getting hungry and ready to go. It was late, so the only decent place to eat this late at night/early in the morning was Waffle House. Tray and I both ordered the All-Star breakfast with scrambled eggs and cheese, grits and sausage with a Sprite. We talked about the club, work, school, music, football and eventually us.

That's when Tray admitted, "I didn't tell Serenity that I was here because I didn't want her to come with me. I wanted to experience this time with you alone because I'm starting to have feelings for you, and I think those feelings are deeper than my feelings for Serenity."

I can't lie, the more time Tray and I spent together, the more and more he gets a piece of me that used to belong to Serenity. Of course, I didn't tell Tray that. Instead I told him, "Okay. We can ride this thing out and see where it goes with me, you, and Serenity."

We finished eating and headed back to my apartment. Tray started watching TV, while I showered and changed into my sleeping clothes. Tray was on the couch with only his boxers on. I took some pillows and sheets out of the hall closet for Tray. I cuddled up on the couch next to him and before long I was knocked out.

Tray's kisses on my neck woke me up the next morning. Tray told me that he had to get dressed because his friends and their families were going to tailgate before the Falcons game. Tray invited me to come but I declined. I needed to get a few things done since this was my only day off for a while. I made up my mind; I was not going to give up my job, especially not for Serenity.

I told Tray about my decision and he was cool with it. "I understood why you don't want to leave. At the end of the day, you need to do what's best for you, not what me or Serenity wants you to do."

After Tray showered and got dressed, I took him downtown to the Georgia Dome to meet his friends. He told me that his friends would bring him back to my house and that he would call before he came. Tray kissed me goodbye and I kissed him back. With every kiss, I swear

he was drawing me in more and more. Tray was a really

great kisser! I could kiss him all day but he had a tailgate

party to get to. When Tray left to join his friends, I decided

to go get something to eat and do a little shopping. I had

been so busy at work that I hadn't even gotten my

Christmas tree and decorations for my house, yet. So I

decided to go to Wal-Mart and get my tree, put it up and

surprise Tray before he came from the game. I decided on

the colors silver and baby blue.

When I got to Wal-Mart, I decided on a seven-foot

pre-lit tree. I got some silver and light blue ornaments and

flowers for the tree as well. While I was in Wal-Mart, I

decided to pick up a few items for the dinner as well. I

planned to cook for Tray, hoping that he would have me for

dessert.

SIXTEEN

TRAY

I have really gotten to know Andrea over this past week. I must say she is extremely fun and funny to be around. Like Serenity, Andrea and I have so much in common, but the connection with Andrea seems so much stronger. I think the reason I'm so drawn to Andrea is because she is such a genuinely sweet person. She's not self-centered or controlling like Serenity. I like Serenity, but, at times, she can get this *I'm better than you* and *if I don't get my way, nobody is going to be happy* attitude.

Nevertheless, I'm not sure if I want to be in a three-way relationship because my feelings for Andrea are starting to outweigh my feelings for Serenity. If I had to make a decision, I would pick Andrea without a doubt. Texting and talking on the phone with Andrea this last week was great. When I surprised Andrea at work with flowers, I saw that she was just as happy to see me as I was to see her. Her actions afterwards definitely said that she missed me too!

The Falcons lost to the Saints 27-24. I texted Andrea to let her know I was on my way to her house. Since tonight was my last night in Georgia, I wanted to spend it with her. Tim was mad because I wouldn't go to the strip club with him, but I just wanted to spend as much time with Andrea as I could before I had to go back home.

I made it to Andrea's house and the smell of food hit my nose, as she opened the door. I walked into the house and I noticed that she had put up her Christmas tree and some other Christmas decorations in her living room. Like Serenity, Andrea went with non-traditional colors in her décor. She chose silver and light blue and with some added white and clear ornaments. Those colors really reminded me of a winter wonderland. It was beautiful.

Andrea had also cooked for me. She made a salad, steak with sautéed shrimp, dinner rolls, loaded baked potatoes, and a homemade key lime pie. She had the table set up with candles and wine glasses; it was really romantic. I grabbed Andrea and kissed her for what seemed like minutes before finally breaking away and going to the bathroom to freshen up before dinner.

Everything was wonderful. Not only was Andrea beautiful, smart, fun, funny, sweet, loving, independent, and caring, but she was also a great cook.

After dinner, we just cuddled up on the couch and watched movies. I couldn't help but get a sense of déjà vu. A couple of days of ago, Serenity and I were doing the same thing, but somehow this feeling with Andrea was much more sincere and stronger than whatever I felt with Serenity.

Cuddling with Andrea was great. We were acting like teenagers, taking silly selfies and pictures. Andrea's phone took better pictures than mine, so we were using her phone. I was trying to take a picture of Andrea and accidentally hit video instead of camera. When I told Andrea, she asked, "Have you ever recorded yourself having sex?"

"No. Have you?"

She giggled, answering, "No."

Light bulbs went off in my head and I told Andrea to let me record her. She laughed at me at first, but when she realized I was serious, she stopped laughing. Andrea got up and went into her room. When she re-emerged into the living room, she was wearing this black lace lingerie with slits up each thigh and black pumps. Even though she didn't tell me to, I quickly grabbed her phone off the couch and started recording her. Noticing that I was recording her, she modeled for me before slowly undressing.

I began undressing as I recorded her. Before long, we both were naked. Still recording, I followed Andrea into the bedroom as she set up a place for me to place her phone, so that it would record without one of us having to hold it. After we got the phone situated, Andrea laid on the bed. I walked over to her and started kissing her all over, from her forehead to her juicy, wet pussy. Instead of taking things slow, I was licking, sucking, and kissing that pussy like I was punishing it. Andrea tried to push my head away but I had her legs spread wide and was holding them open with my hands as my tongue continued to punish her clit. Before long, Andrea starting shaking like an earthquake, but before she could burst, I filled her with my dick and started stroking her at a fast, yet steady pace. It took her a minute to catch my rhythm, but, when she did, she was lifting her butt off the bed to meet me as I plunged in and out of her. Once our bodies fully synced with each other, the sex seemed to intensify.

We switched places and she began riding me like she was riding the mechanical bull at U-Bar, only she didn't fall off. I couldn't help thinking again that this girl was simply amazing. She was taking all of me in her without hesitation. Just as I was about to cum, she stood up over me, turned around and rode me reverse cowgirl style. The way she bounced her ass up and down my dick made me burst inside of her. Andrea got up, turned back around and began to clean up my spilled love juice with her mouth.

When she was sure that it was all gone, she continued to kiss, suck, and lick until I was up and ready to go again. I stood up, picked Andrea up and walked her to the nearest wall, being careful to stay in view of the camera as I drilled my dick into her. That pussy was so good, I burst again within minutes. Good thing I had started walking back to the bed because my legs felt like they were about to give out and I didn't want to drop Andrea. I placed Andrea on the bed and stopped the phone from recording before collapsing on the bed besides her.

We both must have fallen asleep because we both woke up to someone knocking on the door. We both immediately hopped up. Andrea put on her robe and went to see who was at the door. She came back in the room minutes later. "Tim is outside waiting on you so that you all can leave and head back to Mississippi."

I quickly showered, brushed my teeth and got dressed within ten minutes. Andrea kissed me goodbye, saying, "Text or call me." Then she smiled and licked her lips seductively. "I'll send you the video."

The thought of the video made me smile a big old Kool-Aid smile. I kissed Andrea one last time before walking out the door. I hated to leave Andrea, but I knew we would meet again.

Being honest, I just could not wait.

SEVENTEEN

TRAY

Christmas was two weeks away and I decided that I wanted to take Andrea to my family dinner to meet my family. We had been talking non-stop since I got back home. Though she, Serenity and I were still acting as a trio, I was feeling Andrea more than Serenity. I was only communicating with Serenity because I was afraid if I did I would lose Andrea too.

I was ready to make Andrea mine and introduce her to my family but I didn't want to ask Andrea over the phone, so I made a spontaneous trip to Atlanta, just to ask her to be my date at my family Christmas dinner. I didn't tell Andrea anything. I just decided to surprise her. When I made it to Andrea's house, I parked outside and texted her.

Me: COME OUTSIDE!!!!

I guess she thought I was playing games with her.

Andrea: Stop acting silly!

Me: COME OUTSIDE, NOW!

Instead of texting back, I saw Andrea come to the door and open it. When she saw me standing beside my car with flowers and a Christmas gift, she couldn't stop blushing and it looked as if she wanted to cry. I started walking to her because she was standing in her doorway, frozen with shock. By the time I made it to Andrea, she was crying. I wiped her eyes, kissed her and hugged her. We stood at her door, hugging for what felt like forever before we went into the house.

When we got in the house, I gave her the flowers and her Christmas gift. She put the flowers in a vase and sat it on the kitchen table. Then she sat down at the table to open her gift. I got her a Jane Seymour Open Hearts Necklace.

She gasped. "Oh my God, Tray. This is beautiful."

After I helped her put on the necklace, she turned and kissed me.

"Sit down," I said breaking our kiss. "I want to talk to you about the real reason way I made this trip."

Andrea looked hesitant, so I assured her with a charming smile. "Its good news, trust me... Andrea, I want to know if you would like to go to my family's Christmas dinner with me. I guess what I'm saying is that I want you to meet my family. I know it's still quite early, but I really like you and, believe it or not, you will be the first girl I have ever taken home."

Andrea looked confused and before answering my question, she had a question of her own. "What about Serenity?"

"What about her? How long are you going to continue to put your happiness on hold for her? How long are you going to make decisions about your life by worrying about hers? I know you love Serenity, Andrea. I know you do. I care for Serenity too and, before getting to know you, I actually thought I could be with Serenity. But I don't want her, Andrea. I want you! I drove up here to tell you that I only want you! I don't want to share you anymore. I want it to be just you and me; not me, you, and Serenity." I grabbed Andrea hands and asked her once more, "Andrea, will you come to Christmas dinner with me?"

With tears running down her eyes, she looked at me and said, "Yes, I'll go with you, Tray, but I can't pretend as if I don't still care for Serenity, because I do. I probably will always care for her, but I do know that the feelings I have for you and the feelings I have for Serenity are different and that with each moment with you, my feelings grow stronger."

"I understand, Andrea. I'm not trying to pressure you. I just think that it's time for you to live your life and be in control of your own happiness. I know I can make

you happy, if you just give me a chance."

EIGHTEEN

SERENITY

It's Christmas Day and I have nothing planned. I thought I would have been spending it with Tray and Andrea, or one or the other, but they both had other plans. For the last two weeks, Andrea has been real distant and short with me. I can't tell if she is mad at me or just busy. I finally told her how I feel about her and now it's like she is just blowing me off. Like the saying goes, "It's easy to take off your clothes and have sex. People do it all the time, but opening up your soul to someone, letting them into your spirit, thoughts, fears, future, hopes, and dreams; *that* is being naked."

Revealing my true feelings to Andrea got me feeling naked as hell. If this is how Andrea felt all those years while waiting for me to love her then I understand why she was so frustrated with me. It's crazy that I spent so many years hiding my love from her and when I finally do realize my feelings for her, they come at a time when I have feelings for somebody else. Man, I'm in a fucked up situation. My life feels like a blues song, except I don't know how this song is going to end. I'm really starting to like Tray, but I don't want to lose Andrea either. Deep down, I knew I shouldn't have encouraged Andrea to do the threesome/foursome. I knew she felt unsure and uncomfortable doing it, yet I didn't stop it because I wanted it to happen. It was all about me. Now I understand what Andrea was trying to say to me at the mall. I *am* selfish! That threesome/foursome was about me getting what I wanted and I didn't stop to consider Andrea's feelings or Tray.

Tray and Tye are guys, so I knew they would go along with it, but I knew Andrea was uncomfortable with it, but I didn't stop it. Tray must have sensed Andrea's nervousness, because he focused on her way more than he did me. I know he did that to make her feel secure, but it made me mad. Looking back at it now, I'm not sure if I was mad at him for being with her or with her for being with him. Either way, the damage was done because Tray and Serenity have been really distant since then.

Whenever I would text Andrea, I got a one word response. When I would call her, it either went to voicemail, or she would tell me that she would call me back and never would. Tray was either always at a football function or in class.

I got tired of the one-way calls/texts, so I just stopped altogether. That was about two weeks ago. Today is Christmas and I'm spending it alone because I just wasn't in the mood to celebrate. I wasn't in the Christmas spirit. All I wanted for Christmas was *him*. To finally find love and not have to spend anymore holidays alone. All I wanted was Tray. If I could have had Tray *and* Andrea, that would have been a better Christmas gift.

Since I couldn't have either, I called up one of my friends with benefits to come over and spend Christmas with me, since Andrea was preoccupied already.

NINETEEN

ANDREA

I was having Christmas dinner at Tray's parent's house. It was great. Everyone was so nice to me. I got to meet Tray's grandparents, his mother and her new husband, his sister. I already met Tye. It was kind of awkward seeing him again, but he welcomed me like the rest of the family like nothing ever happened between us.

Tray and Tye were so much alike that if I didn't know what Tray was wearing, I believe I would have gotten them confused. His parents and grandparents just couldn't believe that Tray actually brought someone home to meet them. Dinner looked like the scene from the movie *Soul Food*. Tray's family had chicken dressing, turkey, ham, roasted duck, collard greens, green beans, cream corn, mashed potatoes, gravy, macaroni & cheese, potato salad, black eyed peas, sweet potato pie, pecan pie, lemon cake, caramel cake, strawberry cake and lots more.

Being around his family, and seeing how accepting they were of me, I knew that I would never have that with Serenity, no matter how much I loved her or how much she loved me. The things I feel for Tray and the way he makes me feel, Serenity has never made me feel like that. Serenity was always about pleasing herself first, so I would always come second in her life. I refuse to play second any longer, especially when there is someone who wants me to be first in their life. Serenity will always be my friend, but as far as a relationship, it was time to close that chapter in my life, once and for all.

On the way back to the hotel from Tray's parent house, I asked Tray to take me over to Serenity's house. Even though the three of us had still been talking, I was tired of me and Tray pretending and hiding our love in order to spare her feelings. He was leaving it up to me to break the news to Serenity, but I knew that he was getting anxious and tired of pacifying Serenity for me.

"I'm ready to tell her the truth," I told Tray. "I want to do it in person, with you by my side."

"Okay. I have no problem with that," Tray said.

When we arrived at Serenity's house, she must have heard us outside and came to the door. She stood in the doorway, shocked to see us there together.

"H... Hi, y'all. Come on in."

There was an awkward silence as we settled in the living room.

There was no point beating around the bush, so I just decided to get it over with.

"Serenity, I know it's Christmas, and I don't want to spoil that for you, but I just want to let you know that Tray and I are in a relationship. I'm tired of sneaking behind your back and hiding our love from you. Since the day I left and went back to Atlanta, Tray and I have been inseparable. What happened between all of us shouldn't have happened. I was just too afraid of losing you because I loved you so much. I went along with it to make you happy and you never once noticed how uncomfortable I felt, or you did and just didn't care. Tray noticed my sadness and he barely knew me. You've known me most of my life and you didn't even sense how what was happening was making me feel. Serenity, you are a very selfish person. You don't care about anyone's feelings but your own and, until you do, you will always be alone or just kicking it. I'm not trying to be mean and I'm not trying to hurt you; I just want you to wake up and see how the things you do, hurt the people you claim to love. I'm so glad my eyes finally opened long enough to let someone else come along and love me for me, not for what I could do for them or how I can make them feel. Tray truly loves me. Not only does he tell me, but he shows me. I hope that we can still be friends, but that's all I want us to be. I love you, Serenity, but I love me more, and it's time for me to live my life and be in control of my own happiness for once."

Serenity didn't respond right away, but just as she was about to open her mouth, a guy called out to her from her bedroom. "Serenity? Who was at the door?"

She looked like a deer caught in the headlights. Tray's eyes were bulging out of their sockets. The voice sounded familiar. When Serenity didn't answer, the guy walked into the living room. It was TYE! I didn't even bother to let Serenity explain.

"I'm ready to go, babe. Let's go, Tray!"

"No, I'm not going anyway, I want to know what's going on? Tye? Serenity?" Who wants to explain?

Serenity and Tye was speechless. I was pissed and started to walk towards the door, but Tray stopped me. "Bruh, tell me what's up?" Tray said to Tye as their eyes held their own separate conversation.

"Okay, Bruh. It started out as a simple text the morning after and one thing led to another and we been hooking up ever since then," Tye said to Tray.

"Okay, cool. I guess everybody happy now!" Tray said looking over at me. I looked away and for a few seconds, Serenity locked eyes with me and I hurriedly looked away. I'm not sure how I felt about Serenity and Tye, but I was happy with Tray and if Tye makes Serenity then I'm glad for her. She does deserves to be loved as well, regardless of her past.

Leaving Serenity's house, I had no regrets. I did what I came to do and it felt great. I had some doubts about her and Tye, but it wasn't my place to choose for her. For once, I felt the hold that Serenity held over me for so many years being released and erased. I kissed Tray as we walked back to the car and headed back to the hotel. This was a great Christmas and I got the best gift of all. I was in love and I had someone that loved me in return.

***

Tray was ecstatic about the twins. I never thought I would be having a baby, let alone, having two babies. For so long, I went looking for love. I waited years for Serenity to realize how much I loved her and tried to get her to love me in return, but to no avail. It wasn't until I stopped looking for love, that love finally found me! I wasn't looking for love this Christmas, but Love found me!

EPILOGUE

Tray

It's funny how life works out. Life is great. Over a
year and half ago, I never could have imagined settling
down, starting a family, and playing in the NFL. I met two
beautiful, intelligent women and in a crazy sort of way, I
fell for them both. Although, I married Andrea and we have
two beautiful kids: twin boys, Tramiere and Tymiere, we
couldn't push Serenity completely out of our lives. As
much as Andrea tried to bury her feelings for Serenity, I
knew she was still in love with Serenity and being with me
was not going to make her love for Serenity disappear.

After Christmas, Serenity and my brother, Tye
dated for a while, but they broke up after Serenity got
pregnant and wanted him to settle down. Tye liked

Serenity, but he wasn't ready to just settle down, get married, and become a family man.

Tye had a hard time accepting the true nature of Andrea's and Serenity's relationship and decided it was something he wasn't ready for. Andrea' and Serenity's pregnancies helped rekindled their friendship.

Serenity was pregnant with twins as well and gave birth to twin girls, Tamia and Tamoria, a few months after Andrea had our boys, Tymiere and Tramiere.

Tye was active in his kids' lives' but he and Serenity couldn't make their relationship work because Tye just couldn't accept the fact that Serenity was still in love with Andrea.

Andrea didn't want to lose Serenity again. Serenity didn't want to lose Andrea and I didn't want to break up my family by asking Andrea to choose. So, Serenity moved in with us and became a part of the family. She was a wife to Andrea, I just reaped the benefits of their love, but it was clear that her place in this family had more to do with Andrea than me. As long as my wife was happy, then I couldn't ask for more because I know how she feels about Serenity.

Despite everything, I couldn't be happier. Andrea and my babies are the best things that ever could have happened to me and even though Serenity girls' aren't mines technically, I treat them as they are. I'm thankful for Serenity because she taught me a level of love that I never knew existed. A lot of people will not understand our relationship and that's okay, it's not for them to understand. What's understood doesn't have to be explained. None of us expected anything like this to happen, but I love my little polyamorous relationship. We all fix together as pieces of one happy puzzle.

My mother always says, *The Lord works in mysterious ways*! Yes, He does, and I'm so glad His works made me a better man than I was. Even though, Christmas is long gone, just being with my wife, Andrea, my children,

Serenity, and my nieces, makes every day feel like

Christmas morning!

Love is the greatest gift ever. It's even better when

you can love two and the best thing about it is that you get

to open it every day, not just on Christmas!

The End

SNEAK PEEK OF

ILLICIT LOVERS: A TALE OF TWO WIVES

MEET THE WIVES: PLEASURE & KIARA

Dear Diary,

Borrowed time seems to be the best time of my day. Although it's never long, it feels like forever. Crazy how stolen moments with Demetrius means more to me than the time I spend with my husband, Sy'Ere. How can something so wrong, feel so right? How can Demetrius have complete control over my body instead of my husband? The way my body reacts to Demetrius and how our bodies synch when we are near each other without so much as a word is amazing. A simple text from him, makes me wet. I dare not say it is love, but merely lust, but whatever it is; I want this feeling to last.

STOLEN MOMENTS

I heard a quote once that said, "Time is free but it is priceless. You can't own it, but you can use it. You can't keep it, but you can spend it. Once you've lost it, you can never get it back" so I learned to value my time by making each and every moment count, especially the stolen moments with you.

After being apart for so long, our time has finally come

I'm here with you right where I belong

There is no time to waste, for time is not on our side

It will all be over soon and then again you will be gone

Stolen moments are all we have

I'm not yours and you are not mines

But at this moment, it's our time.

After being apart for so long, we are finally together

You kiss me and I feel like I'm floating like the wind
guiding a feather

I fall to my knees in submission

I bow my head in silence

I raise my nates to greet you, they fall open like a broken
heart

Your hands find them and push them back together as if
you trying mend my broken heart

For a minute, my heart is whole and locked again and only
one have the key

You insert your key into my lock to see if you are the one

The one that can unlock the secrets of my heart, the passion
that burns within me, the love that hides within.....

Your key clicks in my lock, a perfect fit

Secrets are released

Memories are relived

Love fills the air all while we embrace this stolen moment

No words are needed, even though there's plenty to say

What's the point? As in your arms I lay, knowing that soon
out time will be done

You have to get back to your life and I have to get back to
my mines

So my heart is locked again and

The key is hidden until the next time I need my broken
heart mended

I wish I could make this stolen moment last

But our time is done, until next time

So, we put back on our masks and get back to our lives all the while reminiscing and waiting on our next stolen moment.......

Watching him sleep, I'm dreading waking him up so he can go home to his wife. Yes, Demetrius is married. Sometimes I feel bad about sleeping with somebody else's husband but then I think about the women that are sleeping with my husband and I don't care. I know that sounds harsh but it's the truth.

Sy'Ere works on the oil rig on the coast so he is only home a couple days sometimes two weeks to a month at a time, which makes it easier for Demetrius to come over most nights. My kids never see him here and I am very, very careful to never let them know I cheat on their father. As far as they know, I'm a great wife as well as I am a great mother.

The outlandish thing about it is that I know my husband Sy'Ere is doing the same thing while working out of town. My husband and I don't have a formal open marriage, but then again we kind of do. I know that he cheats on me and he suspects that I am cheating on him. We have a 'Don't ask, Don't tell policy. We take care of the household and kids and when one of us is out or going to be late, we simply don't ask questions. Again, crazy I know but it works for us. We actually don't argue anymore. Not sure if it's because of the policy or simply because I just ignore his ass. Either way, there is a little bit more peace in our house.

I'll write more later, it's time for me to wake up Demetrius so he can go home to his WIFE!

Kiara

Dear Diary,

Demetrius hasn't come home yet. Of course, he is with her. He is always there. Sometimes, I wish he would just leave me for her and then I could just move on with my life. Sitting here waiting on my husband to leave his mistress is not something that I planned to do in my marriage. If I had known this would be my life, I never would have gotten married.

I know Demetrius isn't in love with me anymore, but some part of him, just won't let me go. Truth be told, my love for him has diminished as well, but I'm not ready to let him go, or maybe I'm just afraid to let him go.

Now, things are escalating. He does not even care if I know he is out cheating. He is just sloppy with it or he doesn't care. He no longer tries to hide that he's with her. It's like he wants to hurt me enough, so that I will finally say, fuck it and leave on my own. I don't understand why he just won't leave me, if he doesn't love me anymore.

YOU DON'T LOVE ME

You say you love me

But your actions say otherwise

If you don't love me, then let me be

Can't you see the tears my heart cries

You don't love me

I'm tired of an empty bed at night

I'm tired of the constant feeling of being alone

I'm tired of not having someone to hold me tight

I'm tired of a house that no longer feels like a home

That's not love and you don't love me

We are not even friends anymore

Neither are we lovers

Loving you has become a chore

I just don't see how this love can ever recover

There is no emotions

There is no passion

There is no affection

There is no love left

You don't love me, maybe you never did

But the sad truth is I don't love you either

I did love you but you caused that love to leave, yet I kept
my true feelings hid

You don't love me

And I don't love you

Everything's out in the open now

No more pretending

No more silence

No more games

The love has ran out

The care is gone

My heart is locked and you no longer have the key

You don't love me and I don't love you so set me free!

My husband been lost interest in me. Not that I'm ugly or anything like that. I guess married life just became too much for him, so he had to find something or somebody to take his mind off of the pressures of home.

I knew right away when he started cheating. He changed. Of course, I made excuses for his behavior and convinced myself it was all in my head and when denial stopped working, I did what most women did and blamed myself!

I figured I had let myself go, so I tried everything I could to make myself presentable in his eyes. I redecorated our bedroom, updated my lingerie collection, invested in Bath & Body works and Victoria Secret products. I even tried spontaneous sex and being more creative with our sex life and nothing worked. I cried a couple of nights about it, wondering how we got to this point. Nothing I tried, worked. So at some point, I just stopped trying and it seems that once I stopped trying, he stopped caring and the disrespect began.

Like tonight, he is out late again. This makes the third time this week. I know he is with that bitch. He's always with her it seems. Shit, I'm starting to think she is the wife and I'm the side chick. Bet you wondering why I'm so nonchalant about it? Well, truth of the matter is that there nothing I can do about it. My husband and I been married ten years, but he has been having an affair with her for eight years.

I try not to say her name out loud. To me she is simply HER, THE SIDE BITCH, THE HOME WRECKER, THE SLUT, WHORE, etc., although I know her government. Her name is Pleasure Johnson. I'm not go hate and say she ugly and ain't shit because I'd be lying. The bitch is cute or whatever a little short maybe about 5'5, dark skinned, thick, curvy girl. She wears her hair natural, and she doesn't wear much makeup. She works at the college as an admission clerk. Crazy thing is the bitch is married herself, but her husband works out of town a lot, so he's rarely home. I wonder do he know his wife is fucking around on him. Shit, I'm sure he does, but he may be like me and just realize it ain't nothing he can do to stop her, especially if he is barely at home.

It's almost four a.m. and Demetrius still hasn't come home. Sometimes I want to just ask Pleasure, *what the fuck are you doing that I'm not doing? Why do my man keep coming back to you?* But that would be crazy as hell. Asking Pleasure that would make her think I'm surrendering or something and I'm not out of the game, yet.

Even though in my heart, I know he is with Pleasure, I can't help but wonder if anything happened to him, car accident or jail. I get up and start pacing the floor for what seemed like hours and just went I'm about to call the hospital to make sure he hasn't been in an accident, I hear his key turn in the door. I make my way back to bed

and pretend I am asleep.

CONTACT PATTI DOSS:

Email: pattiedoss03@gmail.com

Facebook:

https:/www.facebook.com/authoresspattieldoss

Twitter: @MzXquisiteDiva

Other works by Patti Doss:

Somebody Else's Husband, Tammie's Story

Somebody Else's Husband, Too: Persia's Story

Somebody Else's Husband, Again: Rachel's Story

Illicit Lovers: A Tale of Two Wives

Coming Soon

#WCW: A CYBER CRUSH STORY

ILLICIT LOVERS: SECRETS OF A WIFE

TABOO LOVE

AHSND ANTHOLOGY

SOMEBODY ELSE'S WIFE: SHARON'S STORY

ACCEPTING SUBMISSIONS, CHECK OUT

WEBSITE FOR MORE INFORMATION

www.exquisitereadspublications.com

www.ingramcontent.com/pod-product-compliance
Lightning Source LLC
Chambersburg PA
CBHW032012240626
47153CB00003B/1228